The Wrong Turn

By Ben Winter

The Wrong Turn

By Ben Winter

ISBN: 978-0-9992944-8-2

A big thank you to my friend Chris Hagon, author of
"Electric by Night" (to be released summer 2022), for

helping to shape this story and for keeping me accountable.

To my friends April Rose and Kristabell Stansbury who also helped in keeping me accountable.

A thank you to Jeff Chacon, author of "American Badass", a Vegas ZomCom, who inspired me to create a writers group to keep me focused.

To my son Alex who helped with the creation of some of the names in this story.

To my childhood neighbor Julianna who inspired some aspects of the character Atlas.

Improv is a big part of my life. When someone told me that writing a book is like doing improv, I knew it would be easy for me.

There is a game in improv called "First Line, Last Line". In this game the audience gives the troupe the first line of the scene and the last line of the scene. The actors' job is to create a scene that makes sense connecting those two lines.

This book was a giant game of First Line, Last Line.

I knew how I wanted to start the book. I knew how it was going to end. But I didn't know the middle. And it's a good thing too. Because some of the twists and turns even took me by surprise.

To those who think they have a story in them…you do. Just start. You'll be amazed how it comes out.

Table of Contents

Chapter 1

'Fuck you Melvin!'

'Yeah, yeah, fuck you too George.'

'What's the problem this time?' Atlas asked as he entered the room towering over Melvin and George just as he does with every other human he encounters.

'George said that the modifications he made on the lateral thrusters would speed up my turns by 500%,' replied Melvin.

'They will!' shouted George.

'When!?' replied Melvin.

You see, on my ship, the Shadow Puppet, often referred to as the Pup, I have learned to ignore stupid little quarrels like this as much as I have learned to avoid the Splims. Nobody needs to be around for either of those scenarios. So, does it matter that George happens to be the most ingenious engineer in the galaxy? Does it matter that Melvin might be the best pilot I've ever known? Nope. Because at the end of the day, they both think they are better than everyone else, and I wouldn't have it any other way.

As for now, I probably should get up and go to the bridge. We are about to enter the wormhole to make our much-needed delivery to the Farenx Corporation on Xoxbel. You know, so we can eat, pay for fuel, repairs...the usual stuff that a motley crew of spacefaring delivery guys need.

'Roach, status.' Roach is our AI. It's short for Rochester. I love that his voice is British. It makes getting bad news much easier than if it was a voice like mine.

'Everything normal, captain. Including the typical fighting between George and Melvin. We are close to the wormhole entrance. Would you like me to inform Sharon?'

'No thanks. I'd like to do it the old-fashioned way.'

Better grab the XO and head to the bridge. She really hates missing the crazy wormhole mazes we go through. I think it is a control thing. One wrong turn, and you have no idea where you will end up.

I walk to Sharon's room and knock lightly.

'Sharon? You awake?' I said through her bulkhead door.

'Fuck off, Matt!' is all I got as a reply. I really like that she's too the point. Makes it easy to know what she is thinking.

'Wormhole,' is all I needed to say, and I swear, she was just waiting for me to knock on the door to say "fuck off" because the door was open before I finished the word. Sometimes I think she likes to mess with me just because she can. I don't mind. She is fully there and completely reliable when I need her, and second to Atlas, she kicks more ass than anyone else on the ship, myself included. She's a badass.

As Sharon and I enter the bridge, the bickering is still going on between Melvin and George. You thought maybe they were siblings from the way they carry on with each other all the time yet still have each other's backs when it really counts.

'Melvin, how long until we enter the wormhole?' I ask.

'About ten seconds cap.' Everyone turned their heads rather quickly. 'What? You want more warning next time?' He asked like he was confused and didn't see the problem.

'As a matter of fact, yes!' I said expediently.

'Okay, well, then, you need to get George to lay off me when we are getting ready to enter a wormhole.'

Melvin said as though he was the older brother trying to get his younger brother in trouble.

George interrupted, shouting, 'Hey! You may be the pilot but I know how the ship works, so maybe you can just listen to me for once in your life! You can't maneuver the ship like you usually do to get the extra lateral thrust! You have to engage the hydrox-injectors first. This button right here.'

'Don't!!!!!!!!' Melvin shouted at George. But it was too late, we went through the wormhole's entrance just moments before George pressed the button. And instead of taking the correct turn to Xoxbel, we went down a different wormhole path. According to wormhole nav charts where we are headed is strictly forbidden.

And before we even realized what happened, we pop out into a strictly forbidden area of space.

Chapter 2

'And that's why you give us more than ten seconds of warning time, asshole!' yelled Sharon.

'Okay, listen, fuck you all! This wasn't my fault! It was George who pressed the button.' Melvin rebutted while pointing at George.

All eyes turned to George, but he didn't look back. He didn't even respond to the fact that he was being called out. He was stuck staring at the proximity alert and the vizdar output. He looks worried.

'George…' I said. 'I've seen that look before. I don't like that look. That look means something bad is about to happen. What is it George?'

George said nothing.

'George? Did you forget how to talk?' I asked.

Still nothing.

'What the hell George!? Talk to me. Say something.' I said louder and in a frustrating tone.

'Three.' Was all he could get out, and even that was hardly audible.

'What?' Sharon said in a loud voice to demonstrate the level of volume she expected from George.

'Three.' Again, is all he said, but at least we could hear it this time.

'Three what!?' I shouted in anger and confusion.

And I got no response. Again. 'What the fuck is happening right now?' I said. Mostly to Sharon, but definitely loud enough for the entire room to hear.

'George, tell me what three means or get the hell out of the way so we can see for ourselves!' I demanded.

George still couldn't speak but he did move. And there they were. Three ships. In forbidden space.

The vizdar had identified two ships, the Human Space Patrol battleship named The HSP Canvern, a Morlapian Floush (basically a machine built for destruction of just about anything you can imagine), and a third unknown ship.

Before I could even ask, Atlas said calmly, 'a Splim Vayp.'

'A what!?' I asked because I had no clue, didn't know Atlas knew what it was, and because he said Splim in the span of a noticeably short sentence. Most people don't know what a Splim ship looks likes because Splims never leave survivors. Or at least try not to leave any.

'A Splim Vayp.' He repeated. 'It's their version of a war ship. Well, actually, that's the only kind of ship they have. Basically…'

'Enough.' I interrupted. And before I could get another word out, the vizdar and proximity alarms started blaring several warnings including…MISSLES!!!

Before the first two had their guns pointed in our direction, the Splims had fired three slingshot missiles. They shoot these missiles in any direction and then lock onto the target after they are fired. It takes the saying "shoot first and ask questions later" to a whole new level.

'Fuck!' We all screamed at the same time. We scatter for screens, controls, or whatever we can think to do to do something.

'Melvin, get us out of here fast!' I yell.

Of course, Melvin being the best pilot ever, was already working away on an escape before we even identified the Splim ship.

Melvin snapped his head towards George, 'Are you sure those lateral thrusters will do what you said?'

'Now that the hydrox-injectors are engaged, yes. I am positive!' George replied.

Melvin may argue with George all of the time, but he never questions George's work in a crisis. This situation has Melvin freaked and he must be wanting to do something that the ship has never done before because we have like three seconds before those missiles hit us.

And just like that, I'm on the floor. My head is ringing, but we're alive. Melvin shifted our ship sideways faster than ever. Yup, George did make the lateral thrusters more efficient and a lot more powerful. Fuck that hurts. I may have a concussion from that maneuver.

'Remind me to buckle up when the hydrox-injectors are engaged.' I mumbled to the rest of the crew that ended up right next to me. They all nodded in agreement. Roach replied, 'Reminder noted captain.'

'Really Roach, now?' I replied sarcastically. At least the head injury didn't ruin my sense of sarcasm. It's my best trait.

I thought the grav panels would keep us upright no matter what was happening, but apparently, they can't compensate for 500% lateral trust. I'll have to get George to fix that soon.

Before I could get my bearings, Melvin was headed back to the wormhole. And before he moved sideways again, I strapped in as fast as possible. Everyone else took the cue and did the same. It was all just in time too, because right after I snapped the buckle together, another jarring shift to the side nearly broke a rib.

'Damn George! You really supped those puppies up!' Melvin shouted in excitement.

As we pull away, I notice that the Splims have opened fire on the HSP and Morp ships. Apparently they didn't like how the situation was progressing and decided it was best to blow up everyone and everything.

Lucky for us, we were back in the wormhole after a few more seconds. Where we were going, we didn't know and didn't care. We were out of harm's way. For now.

Chapter 3

'Where are we headed Melvin?' I ask.

'Honestly sir, I just started going and really didn't plot a course. For now, I would say we are lost. I'll exit in about five minutes and let you know where we are.'

'Okay. I guess that's better than being dead. Keep me updated.'

'Sir, what the hell did we just witness?' Sharon demanded.

'You tell me. Because what I saw doesn't make any sense. I saw a Human, Morp, and apparently a Splim ship all in some sort of "talk" or "diplomatic formation". And I don't know about you, but the last time I checked we were at war with the Morlapians and Splims.'

'Maybe we are secretly working a peace treaty?' George stated, but he was also asking at the same time, trying to grasp at something that made sense.

'No chance of that happening without Vantatlian representation.' Atlas chimed in. And he should know being our only non-human crew mate and a Vantatlian.

Atlas came aboard as our muscle a few cycles back when he stopped some Morps disguised as Vants on Selam station. We were delivering goods to the Farenx Corporation outpost on that station (totally legit delivery, in case you were wondering). Atlas had been stranded on the station after the Morps attacked his ship. He was the only one to make it off the ship alive. So, when the Morps tried to take the delivery, Atlas noticed their disguises and stepped in to get some sweet, unbridled revenge.

They had holosguises that started to glitch out. Plus, the pattern close to the floor shows through in particular light. Pretty easy to detect actually. That's why nobody uses them to do stupid things like rob someone. Anyway...

You should have seen it. He ripped limbs from bodies. He punched holes through their carapaces. I knew Vants were strong, but wow! It's incredible to watch if you have a strong stomach. If not, you won't see much because you'll vomit in the corner after seeing the bodily fluids spraying everywhere from the massive pressure of a Vant hit to the body of their victims.

He came aboard mostly because he had nowhere else to go, we liked him because he saved our asses, and then he stayed because I am pretty sure he has feelings for Sharon. Whom I think shares the sentiment. But neither one of them seems to want to take action on it. My last "relationship" situation may have something to do with it. I'm sure I'll tell you about it later.

Anyway, Atlas is his nickname. His real name is a pain in the ass to write, say, pronounce, and so on, so we just went with the Greek titan. I mean, he is huge! And he took to it without any protest. So, we have that going for us.

'Okay. True. You would expect a primary party in these wars to be present for peace talks.' I replied.

'The part that doesn't make sense are the Splims. Nobody gets them to lay down their weapons, even for a second.' Melvin chimed in.

'That's the part that doesn't make sense?!' Sharon said sarcastically and with surprise. 'The whole goddam situation doesn't make sense. The Morps should have been shooting at both the Humans and Splims. The Humans should've...you know what…never mind. You all know who should be dead now. Everyone in that circle jerk group of ships. Mutual destruction. Maybe each would have limped their way to the wormhole. But chances are that all three would just be a bloom of rubble in FORBIDDEN FUCKING SPACE!!!!!'

'Calm down Sharon.' I pleaded. 'Yes, it is forbidden. But now I have to wonder why. Who said it is forbidden? I mean, the Pimtims created the wormholes and they never told anyone that any location is prohibited. At least, there is nothing in the records about it. We have human nav charts that were created by the HSP and the Farenx Corp. It was that military contract that boosted Farenx to number one. Maybe the HSP wanted a secret hiding place for secret missions.'

'But then why do the Vants also have it as restricted in their nav charts?' Asked Melvin

'Atlas?' I asked

'I never asked, and they never told me.' He replied. 'But I do think there was some level of collaboration from Farenx Corp. that enhanced our previously lacking nav systems.'

'Okay. So, Farenx marked off that location, at the behest of the HSP, as restricted or prohibited or whatever so that nobody goes there by mistake. One would assume that the HSP and/or Farenx is behind some insidious plan involving everyone but the Vants.' I surmised.

'That tracks.' Sharon muttered.

'Fuck.' Said George.

'Fuck indeed.' Replied Melvin.

'Well, who do we go to about this?' George asked. 'I mean, if something bad is about to happen to our man Atlas and his people, or someone is headed for a huge takeover, we definitely need to tell someone.'

'I could contact my father. He might have some knowledge of what is going on or better yet, a way to stop it before it starts.' I said.

'You haven't talked to your father in years. Only a few times since you "quit the family business" to "make it on your own".' Sharon replied.

'True. But he is the owner of the third largest corporation in the galaxy. That means he has some pull, don't you think?' Yes, my response was a bit sarcastic, but hey, that's who I am. A sarcastic ass. Plus, saying it as matter of fact when everyone knows who my father is would have been a waste of time.

Chapter 4

'Dad. Calm down! I didn't call you to hear the same disappointment story again.'

'Disappointment? You think I'm disappointed? No! I am fucking livid!!! You left the family business, you left the family itself, to do what, to be a delivery boy!!!?!?!? What the fuck! If you just wanted to see the universe, you could jump on any one of the family ships and go. But no. You just have to go and prove something, guh!!!'

'Okay. Thanks dad. Like I said, the same story. Mind if I share a new one you might be interested in?'

'What the hell could you, "a delivery boy" tell me that would be of any interest in my life?' Now you know where I get the sarcasm.

As I explained that we took a wrong turn and saw three ships that should be blowing each other out of existence and that they weren't doing so, my dad's anger changed to intrigue.

'Okay. Yeah. I'm interested in this for sure. For one, if I recall correctly, the Canvern captain, Michael Stitch, is buddy buddies with Farenx's VP, Brolian. Brolian has always wanted control of Farenx. Hell, even Walter (the CEO of Farenx) knows Brolian wants control.'

Walter is ruthless and really does just want ultimate power. He is willing to do just about anything to take over the universe. He is just a plain old jerk when it comes right down to it.

My dad continued, 'If the Canvern is involved it might suggest that Brolian is finally putting things in play to get the top spot.'

And if Walter is a jerk, Brolian is a horrible human being. If you can even call him that. He's more like a leach but with teeth and bad breath to boot.

'Interesting, but that doesn't explain the other two ships. What could possibly get either one of them to not shoot everyone and everything at first site?' I asked.

'Good question. At least your brains haven't completely gone to shit.'

'Thanks dad.' And yes, I said that just short of complete sarcastic ass.

'Ha! Well, I'll have to look into that crazy delegation of ships you saw. Besides, that's the second reason for my intrigue. Getting them to not shoot now is likely to result in them shooting at something else later. I want to make sure I'm ready if they aim at me.'

'Always looking out for yourself. Wow. And while we don't seem to be in any trouble at the moment, we did get away as they were all making it a point to shoot us out of the sky. I'm pretty sure they are going to start hunting us down and destroying us before we can talk to anyone. So, for now the target is me, not you.'

'Well,' my dad said, 'you're talking to me, we are related, and now I'll have a target on my back too. So, thanks for that. But I am glad you did. I'll get my people to look into this as quickly as possible because if there is something to be gained or something to lose, I would like to know about it sooner than later. In the meantime, get your ass to safety. You know where I would suggest you go, but that's up to you.'

'Thanks dad. And, it's not like you don't already have targets on your back. That's just a normal thing in your every day life. This one just might be bigger than any of the other ones.'

'Thanks for the reminder. I have to go. Stay safe. Dad, out.'

I don't know why my dad has to be so lame by saying "Dad, out" every time he ends a call with me. But hey, if it brings him joy, have at it. And if he didn't say it at the end of our conversations, I would definitely think something was wrong.

Chapter 5

'How was your talk with Sheridan, your dad, or whatever the hell we should call that ass hat?' Sharon asked me as I walked into the galley.

'Ass hat, that's a good one.' I chuckle. 'My dad thinks we should hide out on one of the family mining facilities in the ring. He wants to find out what he can about the situation before anything bad happens.'

And then I proceed to tell Sharon about Brolian, Stitch, and the rest of what my dad just shared.

'No wonder your family is third in the corporation rankings. Hiding? Really? You don't get ahead by hiding.'

'I agree, but then again, who am I to say anything about running a corporation?' I snickered. 'No hiding here. We have a delivery to make.'

'Did you tell your dad you were going to hide?'

'I didn't tell him I was or wasn't going to hide. I try to tell him as little as possible. Otherwise he will criticize me no matter the choice.'

'Okay, so, on with the delivery then?' Sharon said with a sigh.

'That's the plan. Maybe we still have time to get it done before getting whacked.'

Sharon just looks at me like I'm insane yet expecting me to continue talking through the lunacy. You know, like the look a parent gives you when you are doing something you shouldn't be.

'Sharon, I know this is a risk. We are going to Farenx territory. And if Brolian and the HSP are aware of who we are, they will certainly know our flight plan, destination, and so on.'

'I mean, it's a pretty stupid move if you ask me.'

'Sometimes stupid pays off. Speaking of getting paid, we better move.'

'Roach, please tell Melvin to lay in a course to Xoxbel.' I continue.

'Will do Captain.'

'So, what DO YOU think will be waiting for us on Xoxbel?' I ask Sharon.

'Nothing but trouble, I'm sure.' Sharon said very sarcastically.

'Do you think we should take steps?'

'You know, we haven't been deceptive in a long time. Maybe we detour and go in with a different ship so they don't immediately blow us up as we enter the system.'

'Good idea.' I said. 'Roach, cancel the last. Tell Melvin we are going to Camp Adleston instead.'

'Sir, that location is not on the nav charts. How can I tell Melvin to go somewhere that doesn't exist?'

'Roach, you have a lot to learn about humans. It's code for a secret location that very few people know about. And I guess, you weren't installed since we were last there. Soon you will be in on the secret. Can I trust you?'

'Of course sir. It's not in my programming to just give information away to anyone who asks.'

'Good. Let Melvin know ASAP. We need to get there quick.'

'Sir, you know I can do many things at once. I told Melvin at the same time I questioned you about the camp's location.'

'I know Roach. That's one of the things I love about you.'

'So, Sharon, what's for lunch?'

'Fuck you sir. I'm not your maid.'

'Ha! I know. I just love seeing your face when I ask things like that.'

Chapter 6

Sometime later we arrived at "Camp Adleston".
Camp Adleston is a lone asteroid that we just
happened to stumble upon in uncharted space. It was
an area between solar systems that just doesn't make
sense to send a ship, a probe, or anything really.

And just as we left it, there was our stash of ships,
weapons, and everything else we would ever need in
the event of an all-out galactic war.

I may have left the family business, but I definitely
didn't leave without securing a few things I might
need. I'm not an idiot. Also, you should know, not
everyone can just get weapons. You have to know
people. Easy enough when you are the son of a mega
corporation CEO.

To get to my little asteroid you exit a wormhole that
doesn't really take you anywhere special (so it's
never used) and then travel a few hours to the
asteroid. Give or take really. It's space. Things move.

The cool thing about this asteroid is that it has a big crevasse in the middle of it and that crevasse is always aimed away from the wormhole. Makes for a really good hiding spot.

We found it when we were hiding from space pirates. Yes, there are space pirates. Well, there were. They are more or less wiped out now thanks to the Human Space Patrol, but every now and then someone thinks they can outsmart the HSP and they try their hand at it only to find out, the HSP is really good at hunting ships down.

We mapped it out, wrote it down, but also kept it offline so that it wasn't hackable. Then we occasionally made stops there to make a space station of our own. Super simple thing. It's mostly three boxes. One with atmosphere for things that need it. One that can stay in vacuum for items that don't. And the third is our docking station and living area in case we need to stay somewhere safe for a while. The docking station can hold five ships. One for each of us. You could say we are planning ahead in case we all need to bug out in our own directions. Or for the stupid delivery attempt we are about to make.

We, and by we, I mean Sharon and I, named it Camp Adleston in a weird way. She had a childhood friend named Adle, that always felt like home. I know. Weird name. And in the nature of how old towns were named, I just added the "ston" at the end to make it seem like a legitimate place. That's how it was done way back on Earth, yeah? Well, anyway…the Camp part of the name happened when we decided to camp out at Adleston while avoiding a group of space pirates. Sharon said, let's camp out at Adleston and I misheard her and said "Camp Adleston?" And then when I realized what she actually said I laughed and it's sort of been an inside joke since then.

Oh, you don't think it's funny? Well, you had to be there. Hence the inside joke thing. Geez. Tough crowd.

Anyway, we decided that it would be best to swap out ships to finish the delivery. Because of how good the HSP is at tracking ships, we definitely don't want to appear in Farenx controlled space with the ship that just saw what we saw. Yeah, they probably will figure out who we are as soon as we make the delivery, so we'll have to be ready for that shit when it hits the fan.

We dock at Camp Adleston and head inside. From there I tell everyone my plan and we start making our preparations.

If nothing else, the next few hours should be exciting, if not deadly.

Chapter 7

'We ready to go Melvin?' I asked.

'Ready as we'll ever be. I still would like to say that this isn't a good idea.'

'Noted.' I pause briefly. Just long enough to make it seem like I was giving it some thought. More than I already have. Appearances and all that jazz. 'Did George make the same upgrades on all of the ships while we were getting things ready?'

'Indeed he did sir. And we even got Roach to duplicate the new information into each ship so that he reminds you to buckle up when the hydrox-injectors are engaged.'

'Good thinking. Thanks Melvin. Let's hit the road.'

'"The Road" sir?'

'Apparently it's an old Earthian saying. I like it.'

'Ok. Random. Starting the undocking sequence now.'

While Melvin did his thing I kept running through the options we have come up with. I don't know if it will work, but I know we must get this thing delivered or we'll be dead in the water with nothing to show for it. Did I really need the money? No. But I don't want the crew to know that it will never be an issue. I want them to have purpose. A destination. A thing to do. If they knew I had money as needed, they would never want to do anything or go anywhere. Except to the bars and brothels. Boring. I want to explore and I want people around me. It's much easier to convince people to do both if there is a common purpose.

'Sharon, you there?' I ask over the radio.

'We are ready to go Captain.'

'Okay. My guess is that this will require some insane timing. Don't guess if or when you should, just do it by the clock, by the numbers, and as we discussed.'

'Captain. This isn't my first Bugspo. I got this.'

For those who don't know the lingo, a Bugspo is like a "rodeo" but in the future there aren't bulls, just giant ass bugs. Same concept though.

'I know you do. I think I say these things sometimes because I am not sure about myself.'

'Captain, you have never let us down. Maybe it's time to stop doubting yourself.'

'Maybe you're right. I'll think about it.'

'Think about it? Maybe stop thinking. That might speed things up.' Sharon's playful tone and yet serious response might be the kick in the ass I need to get us through what is about to happen.

'Okay everyone, let's make this happen. Melvin, hit it.'

Chapter 8

We pop out of the wormhole close to Xoxbel just as
we would be if we weren't afraid of what was
waiting for us. And just as expected, there was The
Canvern. Just hanging out by the wormhole.

On any normal day we wouldn't think twice about it,
they wouldn't think twice about us either, and we
would continue on our way.

But not today. Today they decided to ping us.

'Space craft, designation Alpha Monkey, this is the
HSP Canvern. Identify your system of origin and
current destination.'

Melvin replied, 'HSP Canvern, this is unexpected.
Normally we don't get requests like this from you
guys. Is there something we can help you with?'

'Cut the questions and identify your system of origin
and current destination.'

'Wow, they're unfriendly today captain.' Melvin said
as he turned to me.

'Just do what we talked about Melvin.' I replied.

'HSP Canvern. We came from Selba station and are scheduled to arrive at Xoxbel in about twenty minutes. We are running behind and kind of in a big hurry, so if you don't mind, we'll be on our way.'

'Alpha Monkey, what is your purpose for this visit?'

I jumped on the box before Melvin could. 'Canvern, this is out of line for the HSP. You don't have the right to ask us these questions. We are being polite in answering your other questions, but our business is our business.'

'Alpha Monkey…' and there was static.

'What just happened?' Melvin asked. I shrugged and made that scrunchy face people make when they shake their head quickly when they don't have a clue.

'…Alpha Monkey. This is Captain Michael Stitch. Under Section 2a of the Galactic Accords, when the security of our survival is at stake, we can commander any ship in the galaxy without question. We are extending you a curtesy by asking you these questions. Do not assume you know the law better than we do and do not assume that I will stay nice. Answer the question or be boarded, locked up, and tortured as a conspirator against the HSP.'

"Survival?" What do they think we have that threatens the survival of humanity? I guess we should get ready for a boarding inspection. I said to myself.

'Okay. That escalated faster than expected.' I choked on my words as I said them to Melvin. 'Are you ready to do what we talked about?'

'I am Captain.'

'Make for Xoxbel.'

We pick up speed as fast as possible. Obviously we wouldn't be able to outrun the Canvern, but we would at least start a chase and get us both as far from the wormhole as possible.

The chase didn't last long as they caught us in about two minutes. They started reaching out with their grapple.

'They've latched on.' Melvin said.

As we are being dragged back to their ship, the Pup enters the system.

'Right on time.' I said with a smile.

The Canvern drops the grapple and heads towards the Pup. As they turn to go, we engaged our one and only EMP. And bam! Everything stopped. Us, them, everything. The plan worked. We got the Canvern far enough from the wormhole that the EMP wouldn't affect the Pup when we blew it.

About two minutes later, we get a knock on the door, a hiss of gasses exchanging in the airlock, and a Sharon smiling through the airlock. 'Need a lift?' She said with a devious grin as she laughed.

We got onto the Pup and made our way back to Camp Adleston dragging the Monkey with us. The Canvern will recover from the EMP. And now they have two ships of interest that they will be searching and on the lookout for. Not sure if that's a good thing for us or not. Time will tell.

Chapter 9

Standing in the cargo hold, I start asking questions out loud trying to figure things out.

'Why are they questioning ships? Why not just let all ships but the Pup go about their business? There is no way they don't know that the Pup was the ship that saw them in forbidden space. Right?'

'Right sir.' Sharon said.

'They would really only be looking for my baby. And of course, if they knew what ship they were looking for, they would know what the Pup was doing, where it was, and where it was going. Which means they know we have a delivery to that station.'

'Correct again sir.' Sharon said.

'That's why they were hanging out by Xoxbel. They want the Pup and they knew we were coming. But why question the Monkey?'

'They must want the shipment that is coming to Xoxbel. They didn't shoot at the Pup when it entered, they went after it. They wanted the pup intact because they want what it is carrying.' Sharon added.

'That must be why they questioned the Monkey, they didn't want any ship getting through without finding out what they were carrying first, in case we moved the cargo to another ship. They really do just want the delivery' I added. 'And probably our heads.' I mumbled under my breath.

The crew looked around at each other and at the crate as though they were all trying to figure out the puzzle.

'What the hell are we carrying?' Sharon finally asked.

'Let's find out.' I replied.

Chapter 10

'Boss, you never open cargo.' George said in surprise as I started to open the delivery crate.

'You are right about that George. I don't ever want to know if I am being lied to about what I am carrying. Plausable deniability. I just want to get paid at the end of the delivery. But if The Canvern wants THIS CARGO so badly, and they were talking to two different enemies, then it can only be something bad. And if there is a connection between The Canvern and Farenx Corp, then this delivery certainly shouldn't go to either of them.'

'I agree. Let's open it up.' Sharon chimed in with a bit of excitement in her voice.

'Atlas, would mind doing the hard parts there?' I asked. There are some delivery crates that need machines to open them. Or a really strong green alien. Luckily, I have the strong green kind.

Atlas did his thing and opened the crate. We all stared at it. We all stared at each other. We all tilted our heads to the side. And I'm pretty sure we all said in unison, 'What the hell is that?'

'I guess I better check in with my dad and see what he has come up with. And maybe, just maybe, see if he knows what this is.'

'Don't give him details about whatever this thing is. At least not yet. If it's that important to Farenx, then it would be important to everyone. And I don't want your dad to be an enemy to his own son.' Sharon warned me.

'Yeah. Good point. While I am making the call, see if you guys can figure anything out about this thing.'

'Will do cap.'

I head to my room to make the call. I hope my dad has something of value to share. I hope he doesn't yell at me anymore. I hope he actually takes me serious for once.

'Dad, how are you?'

'Really? You're going to waste my time. Why not just ask me what I know?'

'Now who's wasting time.' I snickered.

'Funny.'

'Anyway. Dad. What did you find out? Because we are in fact, being hunted. And I don't like it.'

'Well, I know you didn't take my advice because you never showed at the mining facility.'

'Yeah. We had a delivery to make. We took a different ship and evaded capture. They definitely want delivery. Not just the Pup.'

'You still have the cargo?'

'Yeah. Don't ask.'

'Fine.' And after a long awkward pause, 'I don't have anything solid yet, but the buzz is that someone found the home planet of the Pims.'

'Wait! What?' I ask with great surprise.

'Yes, you heard me. The elusive planet of the most advanced beings ever to exist.' My dad continued. 'The planet of the beings that want nothing to do with us because we are about as useful to them as ants are to us.'

'Interesting. By the way, what are ants?'

'Seriously! Did you even pay attention in school?'

'I paid attention to Sally. She was worth my attention.'

'And that didn't get you anything in return. She wouldn't even give you the time of day, let alone a date.'

'Thanks for bringing up the past dad. But seriously. I know what ants are. I just like that you think I am stupid. Makes it easier for me. Less to live up to.'

'Wow. Okay. Well, if you survive this, we're going to have to have some serious family counseling.'

'Dad, don't make me laugh. You talk about paying attention and including yourself, but you wouldn't have the time for it. You'd always be out in the hall taking a call, or twenty of them. You wouldn't be doing family counseling for us, you would be doing it because you thought I was defective and that you don't actually need to be involved.'

'Ouch. We'll see.'

'So, anyway, back to the big news. Pimtim's home world. Do you know who found them?'

'No. I don't know who found their world or what their association is to any one group. There is definitely a huge lid on it. Super secret. My spies don't even have the info yet. But, the buzz is that the Farenx Corp knows that someone knows and they want the power of the wormholes for themselves. Which really isn't a shock. I mean, who wouldn't want total control over who can go where and when. Talk about power!!! They are probably going to spend all of their resources to find the source, find the Pims, and then find a way to get the wormhole device or devices or whatever it is the Pims use to manipulate the holes.'

'Does that mean you're going to start in on the power grab?' I asked jokingly but really wanted to know on a serious level.

'If the cards land that way, I would happily take it.'

'Okay. Well, then keep me informed. I have a target on my back now. I'd like to move it away and survive long enough to be rejected by Sally again.'

'Deal. Dad, out.'

Chapter 11

'You were right Sharon. Best not to tell my dad about this thing. He would jump on the opportunity to take it off of our hands.'

I proceed to tell Sharon and the crew about the conversation I had with my dad.

'What if we are carrying the key to all of this?' She asked. 'What if that thing we are carrying is the location of the Pims?'

'I thought of that too.' I said. 'Roach, you have a lot of time on your hands. Did you figure anything out with that thing?'

'Sir. I have analyzed the item and it doesn't appear to originate from Human, Morlapian, Vantatlian, or Splim worlds. My conclusion is that it is a Pimtim device of some kind.'

'Maybe this isn't the location of the Pims but a wormhole device itself. But if that's the case, why would we be delivering it? Why would Farenx have us deliver it from one of their stations to another?' I asked the room, very puzzled.

Everyone looked around trying to figure out the puzzle.

'Everyone, listen up. Does anyone know of anything special about Xoxbel Station? Is it known for anything special?' I queried.

Nothing. Not even from Roach.

'Well, the only logical conclusion is that whatever this is, us Humans can't do anything with it, at least not yet. And something on Xoxbel might have changed the game. Maybe they have some advanced research tech on Xoxbel.' Sharon said.

'And maybe they used us because other players are starting to suspect what Farenx has, I mean had, in their possession. Use a lesser-known courier instead of their own ships. And, if things went sideways, they could blame your dad's corporation because you are his son.' George added while looking at Matt to ensure Matt understands the possible ramifications.

'Well, shit. If that's the case, then we are carrying the hottest device in the existence of humanity. Everyone would take a shot at us if they knew we had it.' Melvin said.

'I really fucking hate the Farenx Corp right now.' Sharon added.

'What's our best move boss?' Atlas asked.

'Our best move is to find the Pims and give this device back to them. They are the only ones I would trust with such technology.'

'I guess the only question left is, how do we find the Pims?' Sharon asked.

'The answer is to find the person who knows where the Pims are.' I stated.

I knew that my only connection to this riddle was through my father. But as soon as I ask, he would suspect me. Does that matter? Should I ask anyway? Would my own father turn on his only son? What to do? Or, there was someone else...

'If there is someone who might know, I bet it's my dearest friend.' I said as sarcastically as possible.

'Oh, goodie. Let me leave the room first. That guy is a jackass.' Sharon said as she stood up. 'I don't want to throw up.'

Chapter 12

'Kip!' I said as he popped up on the screen.

Kip, short for Kiping, was my only friend growing up. As you might imagine, growing up rich, you have very few choices in friends. Either the people that just want to use you for your money, or other rich kids. And being that my dad is the number one guy in the Berent Group, oh, did I forget to mention the name of my dad's company, well, it doesn't really matter, my only real friend was the son of CEO, Darvell Spax, of the Weavel Corporation.

To keep you on track, we have the Farenx Corp, Weavel Corp, and Berent Group. Numbers one, two, and three in terms of size of companies and influence in the galaxy.

And in case you were wondering, the number one guy at Farenx, Walter Polues, does have a son and a daughter, but they were way older than either Kip or I so we never really hung out.

Anyway, here was Kip. As happy and annoying as ever. 'Matty Batty, how are you bud!?'

'Still with the nickname huh?'

'You know it! I'll never let that one go. Best night of my life. I got to destroy stuff just like you but never got the blame. Thanks for that, by the way.'

Matty Batty. You know how I like old Earth idioms, right, well, I also have, I guess had, a bat from the old Earth sport called baseball. I got drunk and started hitting random things at a party back in high school. Remember, I came from a wealthy family, so things meant nothing to me. Not even the price tag associated with them. Needless to say, my name sort of changed for a while since Matt and Bat rhyme and when you say Matt went Batty it sort of just morphs into Matty Batty. Anyway…

'I mean, once you die you won't have it anymore, so I have that going for me.' I said.

'Funny. What's up? How's Sharon? She's single right?'

'Well, Sharon left the room when I said I was going to call you so she wouldn't throw up. I'm guessing that means you don't have a chance. As for me, I was in the proverbial neighborhood and thought I would say hi and see how the new gig was treating you? Also, is your dad still pissed at you like my dad is at me?'

'Oh yeah. He always lays into me whenever we talk. I imagine it's the same for you.'

'Sure is.'

'Bummer about Sharon. Oh well, I think I'm great and she is totally missing out on something amazing. Nothing worth gagging over.' Kip laughed. 'The gig is great. I have seen some amazing new places. I almost thought I discovered a new speci….ummm…never mind. I can't talk about that. Sorry. Sometimes I forget that some of my work is classified, and I can't tell people about it. Stupid secrets. Anyway, there are so many branches in the wormhole system that mapping them all is insane.'

'Don't worry about keeping secrets. I get it. I mean, how many secrets do the two of us have about this galaxy given we are part of two thirds of the corporate powers in it, huh?' I asked.

We both laugh about this fact. But it is true. We have seen and heard so many "secrets" in our lives that we sometimes forget what we can and cannot share with others. That was part of my reasoning for leaving the family business. Too much to keep track of.

Also, I definitely caught the word slip. Did he find the Pims? Was it him? Do I even need to keep looking? I need to find out more, but I still need to be careful on my end.

'That sounds crazy. Have you ever been lost?' I continued.

'Sure. We popped out of one wormhole and usually where you pop out you can pop right back in. But no, not in section 81…wait…crap. Almost slipped again.'

'So, not all wormhole exits are also an entrance?' I asked.

'Yeah. I can share that much. It's not like we find them everywhere. Just seems to be the one occurrence so far. But it certainly freaked us out. We have had to come up with a whole new charting program just to handle it in case we find another instance.'

'That would be freaky. Talk about feeling lost. How long did it take you to find a new entrance?'

'Well, that's just it. We couldn't. Crap. Getting me to talk about classified stuff again. No no no Mr Batty. Not this time.'

'Hey, I'm just curious. Not like I have anyone to tell.'

'Enough about me. Why did you really call me? You never just call out of the blue. You always have a reason.'

'You actually have spilled enough information that anything I wanted to know has already been said. At least enough to figure it all out.'

'What?' Kip asked with a brief and worried pause, 'What are you talking about?'

'Look, I can't stay on here very long. We're being hunted. And I am pretty sure you are somewhat responsible. And if not responsible, involved for sure. Your "slips" have more or less proved it.'

'Dude. What exactly are you saying?' Kip looked very worried. 'How am I responsible? How am I involved?'

'I'm just saying that where you have "been" and what situation my crew and I are in right now, might be linked.'

'Then you have no idea what you are involved in, do you?' Kip said seriously. As serious as I have ever heard him before

'I have AN idea. But if you have more information that will keep me from getting killed, I would love to hear it.'

Kip stared at the screen for a short while, and as he was about to start talking, the door behind him blasted off its hinges. A crew of HSP personnel came running in and the screen went black. Kip may have been my only link to the Pims and he was now in the hands of the HSP.

'Fuck!' I said aloud.

Did I mention the HSP is really good at hunting people down? Pretty sure I did. How Kip wasn't already in custody is beyond me. Maybe he was allowed to do his job to possibly find more Pim settlements as long as he kept his mouth shut. But here he was, talking to me. And now the HSP is going to think I know things. Fuck fuck fuck. I'm pretty sure I am going to get myself and my crew killed.

Fuck.

Chapter 13

Standing in front of the crew, 'Okay everyone, here's the plan. We are going to leave the device at Camp Adleston. We are each going to take our own ships. We are then going to go into the wormholes and search for the Pims. Kip said section 81 something. How many holes could there be with at least that much information?'

Without missing a beat, Roach chimed in, '6,766,553 possible routes. And that number grows as exploration continues.'

'How the...?
What the...?
FUCK!!!!' I shouted. 'This just keeps getting worse.'

'Sorry sir. There are just too many sections that start with 81. From there the number of wormhole options just keep going up. The wormhole nav system has only mapped out 0.000001% of the possible wormhole destinations.' Roach continued. 'And that number changes as the system itself is ever changing. The universe is really big.'

'That's enough Roach. You're depressing me.' I said.

'With so many options it doesn't make sense to have a manned crew doing the mapping. It would make more sense to have millions of probes going out and reporting back their destinations.' George stated.

'Yes, that is what happens. Only when something is undefined or "weird" does a manned crew go looking.' Roach explained. 'Or if the probes find new planets, especially habitable ones.'

Melvin had a thought. 'We need to find those anomalies that require a manned crew. That would narrow down the search.'

'How do we do that? Who would we go to?' Sharon asked.

'I don't know right now. Even if we knew how, the info is probably classified beyond top secret. What I do know is that we need to start moving things from fucked to not so fucked. Change things to being more in our favor.' I said.

I continue… 'Atlas, I think it's time to bring in the one species that hasn't been a part of this new revelation. I think we need to go talk to some Vants.'

'Do you have any connections to someone high up who might like to know what is happening?' Sharon asked.

'Our culture doesn't work the same as yours. I can get a message as high up as I want and it will be heard. The timing of it, well, that's where it gets weird. It could take minutes or months.' Atlas replied.

'Well, no better time than now. Let's get a message sent telling your people what we saw. Let's not mention the device, just everything else.' I chimed in.

I follow Atlas over to a communications console.

Atlas sends the following message.

"To the rulers: It has become clear that there is information that affects our people I must share with you today. My crew and I accidentally ended up in forbidden space as we took a wrong turn in the wormhole system. We witnessed a Human, a Morlapian, and a Splim ship in formation, not attack formation, but diplomatic formation. Being that we are at war with two of the three species, and that our ally was one of the ships, this alone is enough to ask questions.

However, additional information suggests a much larger plot. We have also been made aware that the home world of the Pims has been discovered. And

*that the one person we know who was involved has
likely been captured and/or killed.*

*I wish you to know this information so that you are
not caught off guard. I also wish for your assistance
in finding the man who knows of the Pims location.
His name is Kiping Spax and he is the son of the
Weavel Corporation CEO, Darvell Spax. He is
friends with my captain, Matt Ryrer, and we are
concerned for his safety."*

'Good enough?' Atlas asked.

'Better than good. This should get them to take action
immediately. It will likely stir up a hornets nest.' I
replied.

'Sir, you are using old Earthian terms again.' Roach
interjected.

'True, but those are the idioms I love to use.' I said,
you guessed it, sarcastically.

'Anyway, let's get back on track. Until we or they
find Kiping, we have to stay out of harms way.'
Sharon stated.

'Maybe we stir up some more "hornet's nests" cap."
George said.

'What do you mean George?' I asked.

'I'm guessing The Canvern isn't acting on behalf of
the HSP but on their own. What if we got the HSP

involved so that they can investigate their own?'
George replied.

'But if the entire HSP and the Human Government IS
involved, then we would be in deep shit.' Sharon said
mockingly.

'Let's get some more information first. Let me touch
base with my dad.' I interjected.

Chapter 14

'What the fuck do you have on your ship?'

'Nice to see you too dad. What exactly do you know?'

'Well, the HSP rarely puts out a bounty on anyone. But there is one for you and your ship. It's a billion credits! I'm ready to turn on you. Oh, and that's if you are caught dead. It only goes up from there if you are alive and with cargo.'

'Wow. Can I turn myself in?' Yup. Sarcasm is my coping mechanism. 'Seriously though, dad. What is happening?'

'You answer me first and then I might be able to put the pieces together.' He demanded.

I give in. It is probably best to have an ally who knows stuff. 'Fine. You win. We seem to have a device that isn't Human, Vant, Morp, or Splim in nature. That leaves it as a Pim device. Likely a wormhole generator. But we also determined it likely that we were transporting it from one Farenx facility to another because they couldn't get it to work. We think they used us to move it because the rumblings are out there and they didn't want the shipment to get hijacked. Or, to blame you if it did.'

'…'

'Dad. You are never this silent. What are you thinking?'

'…'

'Dad, you're frightening me.'

'Sorry. I just got word that the HSP has one of their ships in our mining colony territory. Which means they do suspect me as a coconspirator but can't act on it yet. I can't be tracked talking with you or they will have cause.'

'Well, that answers the questions of who is involved and who we can trust. Nobody. Fuck, this just keeps getting worse.'

'Watch your language!'

'Dad? Really? Still?'

'Once a dad always a dad. Deal with it.'

'Fine. I need two things from you and then I might be able to solve all of our problems. We need to find Kip. He and I were talking and then we were interrupted when the HSP blew his door in and the screen went blank.'

'Why do you need Kip?'

'We are pretty sure he knows the location of the Pims. If we can get that, we can take the device back to the Pims and then we can end this before it really gets started.'

'And the second thing?'

'Yeah, that. We need to know why the HSP, Morps, and Splims weren't blowing each other up.'

'I'll see what I can find out. In the meantime, just stay hidden.'

'Will do. Thanks dad.'

'Dad out.' And then he hung up.

Chapter 15

'Maybe it's time we go on the offensive.' Sharon said after I recapped the conversation I just had with my dad.

'We need to interrogate some HSP guys. Get something to work with.' She continued.

Sharon used to be Bug Sweat. It's kind of like Special Forces in that it is super-elite and very effective. It's called Bug Sweat because it's always present, hard to detect, and annoying as hell when the heat is on. And boy were they good at putting the heat on the enemy.

I guess you are probably wondering how Sharon and I know each other if I am just some rich kid and she is Bug Sweat.

Well, we were introduced about ten years ago when she was assigned by my father to "watch my ass" as I was learning the family business. The part the public doesn't know, the shady secrets, the business takeovers that were designed to look like a choice when it really wasn't, and basic shit cleanup detail was really why she was assigned. The stuff the public doesn't know is one of the most covert wars you could imagine. Corporations going after each other as well as governments. If you were a spy for the government, you definitely had a higher paying job waiting for you when you were ready. Corporations are wise to let the government pay for the training and then higher the spies after they have proven themselves on someone else's dime. Business is business. Except when it's war.

Sharon had just "retired" from the military. Yes, it was forced. I mean, how many superiors do you have to hit in the face to have yourself "voluntarily" removed from service? At least ten. Although that number might have changed after Sharon's tour of service.

Anyway, she had the skills and security clearance my dad wanted. Easy higher.

We got along okay. It didn't take me long to get that when she said something she meant it. She definitely wasn't couth, and she definitely didn't fluff it up for me.

It wasn't until I had to save her ass that things changed. And how can I save her ass when she is better at just about everything? Money. Duh.

She got into some gambling game on Quant and thought she could win with a Triple Wanderer. I know right!? What was she thinking? Anyway, it was a three million credit mistake.

Pocket change. For me at least. The alternative was a five-year tour of the worst brothels on the planet and she would have been the "main event". And, let's be honest, that five years would have turned into a life sentence because every patron she would hit, or kill, would have added to her time in the system.

I got her out. Paid her debt. She's been forever grateful, although you would never actually hear the words come out of her mouth.

When I told her I was leaving the family business to do my own thing she sent a letter of resignation to my dad on the spot. Okay, it was a two-second phone call saying, "I quit." But a letter would have been the better thing to do.

After she quit she asked if I was hiring for my new adventure. I hadn't even told my dad that I was leaving, but I probably did need some protecting as I went out on my own. Especially after telling my dad. He has a temper.

I don't know if it's my charm or if she still thinks she owes me, but I am glad she has stuck around this long.

'So, who do you have in mind?' I ask.

'The HSP has some lightly guarded stations just outside of some key wormhole exits. Typically setup to keep an eye on our enemies.' Sharon responded. 'I was thinking we head for the one right inside of Morp space. The Morps were involved in that fucked up group of ships. Maybe someone on that station knows some fucking details we might find useful.'

'Sounds good to me.' I nodded. 'Anyone object?'

'Full body armor.' Atlas demanded.

'Um, I've never been in a situation needing body armor.' Melvin chirped.

'You'll be fine.' I said

'Just stay between Atlas and me and you'll be safe.' Sharon said very confidently.

'Standard HSP security systems?' George asked Sharon.

'Yeah, why?' Sharon asked.

'Just need to know what gear to get ready.' George smirked as he replied.

I've never really seen George that excited before. He must know what we will be coming up against, and since he is an engineering genius, he is probably excited for the tasks ahead of us.

The story of George, well, that's pretty simple. I did the stupid bit of sleeping with our last engineer. She was super awesome at her job and we got along great. The sex was amazing. And all was going well until I found out she was married. She didn't like her husband and hadn't seen him in years, but after I found out, things just got awkward on the ship. And after a month of the awkward we all agreed it would be best for her to move on.

Fortunately for her and us, there is an engineering hiring system called EnSwap. Engineers are an awkward bunch. Sometimes they just don't fit with a particular crew. She put herself as available when we got to Orco Station. Pretty big station. She won't have trouble finding a new gig. And I didn't feel the need to add anything to her file keeping her from getting employed with another crew.

Now that we parted ways and needed an engineer, we did a search. For a male engineer, to keep my pants on, so to speak. There were two on station. George and Marcus. Marcus had a temper, according to his last crew. Captain Frew made specific mention of that fact in Marcus' file. A temper would spell disaster if he mouthed off to Sharon. Then there was George, an arrogant yet talented engineer who liked to solve problems in his head before saying anything out loud. He never wanted to be wrong.

Perfect. Neither do I. And if he thinks before he speaks, that will keep him from getting punched in the mouth by Sharon. And that's how he came to be part of the crew. Standard EnSwap engineer hire. Not sure why he was available. That part was left out of the logs, but I don't care. I got a great engineer out of it.

We all scatter to take care of last-minute details, getting our gear on, and of course, helping Melvin with his gear since he didn't really know what to think. Sometimes I wonder how Melvin got to be so good at flying without being part of the military.

Once we were ready, or as ready as we could be, we discussed the plan and hit the road. Yes, I know. Earth idioms. You gotta use what you got.

Chapter 16

'FIVE MINUTES CAPTAIN!' Melvin shouted.

'Melvin, calm down. I'm right next to you.' I said.

'Sorry sir. I am just so anxious, scared, worried, shaky...' Melvin murmured.

'Melvin, calm down. This isn't the first time we have done something stupid together. What's different this time?'

'Well sir, I have flown into crazy situations for sure. But I have never left the ship while on mission. And I've never had to wear body armor. And, well, I've never held a weapon, let alone used one. Except of course for ship to ship weapons.'

'If all goes according to plan, you won't have to use one.'

'All to plan. Got it.'

'Melvin, just breathe dude. We need to do this or we're definitely going to be hunted down and killed anyway.'

'Thanks sir. That's reaffirming.' Melvin replied sarcastically. I guess I'm wearing off on my crew after all. Yes! Goal!

Melvin. What a weird guy. Best pilot I know. Yet he isn't ex-military. I vaguely remember him talking about his past when I first met him on Bloumbome. I wasn't really paying attention. I guess I'll have to ask him someday.

I realized by the time Sharon and I got to Bloumbome, on our first delivery, that we couldn't run the ship and pilot it alone. We needed someone else to be just the pilot.

We walked into the local bar and sat down as you normally would at a bar. Only, we apparently sat down in the seats that some locals always sit in. Needless to say, they didn't like us sitting there when they walked in and started to mouth off at us. I wasn't worried. I had Sharon with me.

'Hey fuckos!' One local guy shouted. 'Get the fuck out of our seats!' I'll call this guy Mark. Mostly because he put a mark on his face for Sharon to punch just by being an asshole.

I saw Sharon tense up out of the corner of my eye. Wrong move fellas. 'What ever do you mean?' I said like I was clueless as to what was going on.

BAM!

'What the fuck!?' I said, not knowing what just happened. There I was getting ready to talk this guy down, and then he was face first on our table, and glass was everywhere. A bottle had been thrown from across the room right into the side of the guy's head.

The other local guy. I'll call him Ted. He looked like a Ted. Ted spun around and locked eyes with the bottle thrower. Before he could start walking, Sharon kicked out his knee. He fell backward and hit his head on the table next to Mark. I guess they really did want this table after all.

Sharon and I got up and walked over to the bottle thrower.

'I take it you know these two fine gents, Mr. Bottle Thrower?' I asked the guy.

'Names Melvin. And yeah. They make this bar less tolerable than it already is. I had always wanted to hit them in the head. It wasn't until I saw her tattoo that I knew the numbers were in my favor. I have a keen eye. I'm a pilot.'

I turn to Sharon and raise my eyebrows a few times in excitement.

'Very nice to meet you Melvin. My name is Matt, and this is Sharon. And I just so happen to be looking for a pilot.'

'All the way out here?'

'Yes. I just started a delivery business of my own and didn't realize just how much I needed a dedicated pilot until Sharon and I almost killed each other on our way here.'

'Not like you would have done any damage to me.' Sharon chimed in.

'Thanks for the reminder.' I replied.

'Well, Matt. Sharon. I just so happen to be looking for a job. I guess the odds must be in our favor.' Melvin said as he stood up. 'And you're in luck captain. I'm assuming it's captain.'

'It is.'

'I just happen to be the best pilot.'

'Best pilot, as in the best human pilot?'

'The. Best. Pilot.'

'Well, Best Pilot Melvin, I guess you're going to have to show us what you can do.' I said with a sense of joy in my voice.

'Let's go.' Melvin said.

'Uh, you've been drinking. I don't think that's a good idea.' Sharon said.

'Well then, if I dazzle you when I have been drinking, imagine what I can do when I'm sober.' Melvin quipped back.

I like this guy.

Melvin proceeded to take us out of the docking station, around the moon, did some crazy maneuvers I have never seen, and then did the fastest docking procedure I have ever witnessed. I'm kind of shocked my dad didn't have this guy locked in for his own uses.

'Alright, Melvin. You've convinced me. We leave first thing in the morning.' I said as I reached out my hand.

'Melvin Donovor at your service. See you in the morning captain.'

And with that, we had our pilot. Ever since he has been a steadfast crew member who I would trust at any turn.

Chapter 17

Just before we pop out of the wormhole at Delta Tango 6118, we launch a jamming probe. Delta Tango 6118 is the designation for the space before Morlapian space, or, for the HSP, the place where they can spy on their enemy's movements.

The jamming probe we sent through first should keep the HSP from identifying us as we pop out of the wormhole and keep them from sending any signals out for help. They will definitely suspect something, so that's the only drawback of using a probe.

I'm pretty sure I mentioned that I stockpiled supplies before going out on my own. Being the son of a mega-corporation CEO has its perks.

We pop out of the wormhole shortly after the probe.

'How long until we dock Melvin?' I ask.

'With my skills, sir, twenty seconds.'

'And, hypothetically, if I were to dock us, how long would it take?' I just want to keep his mind occupied for a few more seconds, at least so the dread doesn't kick in.

'Sir, really? You know you suck at docking. It would take like ten minutes.'

'Just checking. I know you're the best, so make me proud.'

And bam. We were docked.

'George, you're up!' Sharon shouted.

George headed for the door and opened our side of things. From there, he started busting out all his gadgets. Before I could really grasp what he had with him, the HSP docking door was opened, and we were in in less than ten seconds.

'We are in sir.' George said.

'On me.' Sharon said

Everyone follows Sharon as Atlas brings up the rear.

We head for the control room so we can keep requests for help to a minimum or, hopefully, completely silent.

First encounter!

Before I even saw the guy, Sharon had hit him in the head with the butt of her rifle. We all walked by and Atlas kicked him hard in the head to keep him down.

There is surprisingly little resistance as we keep moving forward. An occasional guy caught off guard and now a lump on the floor.

I hear something coming! Shit! I turn around only to see a leg sweep by Atlas. The guy rounded the corner and then saw stars as he turned horizontal and hit the ground flat as a pancake. I'm glad Atlas is on our side.

Atlas doesn't take chances. He ripped the guy's helmet off and bashed his head into the ground to keep him down.

We keep moving forward.

Commotion! I hear what sounds like the thud of two bodies hitting each other. I turn around and see that someone actually snuck up behind Atlas and jumped on his back.

Before I even realized what I was seeing, Atlas threw the guy over his shoulder like he was throwing a towel onto a bench. The guy flew through the air, over my head, and as I turned, I see Sharon instantly change his trajectory into the ground with a kick to the chest. Yes, as you imagined it, she lifted her foot above her head, and at the exact moment, kicked down with such force that this guy never had a chance to lose his breath from hitting the ground. It was already kicked out of him.

In shock, I finally close my mouth and continue following Sharon through the halls.

Finally, we make it to the control room door. We huddle around to make sure we all get through quickly to take the room by surprise.

'Ready?' Sharon whispered.

Everyone nods.

'1, 2, 3' and Sharon pressed the button.

Nothing. The door didn't open as it should.

Fortunately, we have George.

'George. Do what you need to do to get this door open. Just do it quietly.' Sharon whispered sharply into his ear.

George got in position and started to work his magic. We wait. Exposed, with a trail of lackies from our ship to ops.

'Footsteps.' Sharon whispers to Atlas.

Atlas spins around and heads to the edge of the wall. Just as the guy comes around the bend, he breathes in to yell for help and his exhale comes from Atlas' punch to his gut. Before the guy could throw up, Atlas hit him again in the head. Out cold. Atlas kept him from hitting the ground hard and eased him down to the ground.

As Atlas approached our group again…

'It's ready.' George finally whispered.

'Let's hope they didn't hear us or see us coming.' Sharon whispered to nobody in particular.

She pressed the button and the doors opened. We all rush through and...

BAM!!! Before we could all get through, Melvin is hit with gunfire.

'Shit!!! Melvin's been hit!' George shouts.

Sharon took a shot at the shooter in return. She didn't leave much to interrogate. The dude's head is now gone. But the effect worked. Everyone else in the room, seeing Sharon, Atlas, and the shooter's head pretty much everywhere, they all started to lay their weapons down.

I guess they didn't care that I was also there aiming my weapon at them.

George put his gun down to check on Melvin.

'Melvin?' George spoke with great anticipation.

George continued to shake Melvin a couple of times. He looked up at me and looked worried.

'Melvin!' George shouted. 'You fuck! You better not die on me!'

Melvin jerked ever so slightly. Put a smirk on his face and mumbled, 'Fuck you too George.'

'Asshole.' George said in return but clearly as lovingly as possible.

'I guess the body armor was the right call. Thanks Atlas.' Melvin said as he started to pick himself up.

'So, Sharon. Now that that drama is over, who do we start with?' I asked.

'Him. Mr. CO over there.' Sharon replied.

Chapter 18

'I'm not in charge!' the CO demanded.

'Then who is?' Sharon asked.

'The guy you shot?' he replied.

'Right. I noticed his uniform. He outranks you. But since he is now dead, that makes you the commanding officer.' Sharon said and then continued sarcastically, 'I'm surprised you didn't know that.'

'Yeah…Right…Got it…I'm just…just…ummm…Are you going to kill me?' he asked.

'Listen, what's your name?' Sharon asked as though they were becoming friends.

'Peter.'

'Listen Peter. I may have to kill you. But that largely depends on what you know and even more so, what you tell me.'

'That…seems…fair.'

'For second in command, you really should be a little more…resistant.' Sharon said. 'But I'm glad you're not. Cause that will make this easier for me.'

'Sit!' Sharon demanded.

'George, tie him up really good.' Sharon continued with her orders.

'I should warn you that I don't know anything.' Peter said as though it would help.

'But you don't know why I am here. So how do you know you know nothing?'

'Good point.' Peter said as he looked defeated.

'Now. Tell me where you keep the K131s!' Sharon said.

Sharon's got her tactics from the best. So, it's best not to question anything she asks during an interrogation. Even when you have no idea what she is talking about or where things are going. Like K131s. We have no use for them, nor were we looking for them. Oh yeah, you probably don't know about them. They are big-ass missiles that destroy ships with little to no effort. Standard issue for the HSP.

'The K's?' Peter asked in a confused voice. Eyes darting from person to person, looking for clarity.

'Yeah. Duh. Why else would we be here?' Sharon said in a mocking tone.

'Uh, because, wait, aren't you guys from the Shadow Puppet?' Peter asked like some light went on.

'The what?' Sharon asked like she hadn't a clue.

'We were told to be on watch for the Shadow Puppet. It's a ship of interest.' Peter said. 'And then you showed up. Seems like anything but a coincidence.'

'I'll keep an eye out for the "Shadow Puppet" and let you know if I find it.' Sharon said sarcastically.

'Well, if you aren't the Shadow Puppet crew then who are you?' Peter demanded.

'Does it matter!!' Sharon 'We want the K131s!!'

Sharon looked back at me and winked. She has him right where she wants him.

'I don't have access!' Peter said as though his life depended on it. 'You shot the only guy who did!'

'Well, that isn't going to help you now is it!' Sharon yelled. 'If you can't get me access, then I have no reason to keep you alive!' Sharon pulled out her gun and held it to his head.

'No! I have information. Valuable information. That's what I can offer! Just don't kill me!' Peter cried.

'What kind of information!?' Sharon demanded. 'Tell me now or it's bullet time!'

'Information that could change the war!' Peter shouted. 'I know things about the war that most people don't. That's why I was stationed here. To keep an eye on the enemy and to keep the knowledge compartmentalized.'

'What good is that information to me!?' Sharon yelled louder than ever.

'Maybe if you hear it, you'll find a use for it! Just don't kill me!!!!' Peter was in tears at this point.

And Sharon had the biggest smirk on her face. She had won. She had gotten him to share without even hinting that she wanted this exact information.

'Maybe.' Sharon said in a lower voice. 'Start talking, and if the information doesn't work for me...' she tapped the gun to his forehead a few times giving him the idea that it better be good or he will be dead.

'Okay, but first...' Peter started to say in his still scared little boy voice.

Chapter 19

'Let's cut the bullshit, shall we?' Peter said in a completely different tone of voice and physical demeanor. 'I know who you are Sharon Marshfield of Bug Sweat Unit Echo.'

Sharon's eyes went wide as she looked back at me.

Peter continued... 'I know YOU ARE the crew of the Shadow Puppet and I let your asses make it to the control room.'

'You let us?' Sharon asked, puzzled.

'Yes. I DID. Not the guy you killed. Me.'

'So, who are you, Peter, if that's your real name.' Sharon asked sarcastically.

'Yes, Peter is my name. Don't let the rank on my uniform confuse you. I am in command of this station. And I was stationed here for two reasons. And, if you untie me, we can actually have a civil fucking conversation that will be mutually beneficial.'

'Well, I'll need a little bit more before I just untie you.' Sharon retorted.

'Sharon, what do you know about Designation 13?'

'I know it is a secret group of assholes that seem to operate in the shadows, only nobody can prove they exist, even Bug Sweat.'

'Minus the asshole part, you are correct.' Peter said. 'And while I still won't confirm it, you can probably put the pieces together from here.'

'Fine. Cut him loose if he isn't already free and just being polite.'

'Good call Sharon. I am in fact, being polite. I ask that you do the same and untie me.'

Atlas stepped in and cut the bonds but also kept a hand on Peter's shoulder just to make sure he didn't do anything stupid.

'Okay Peter. You are free. Start talking.'

'Hmmm…where to start?'

Chapter 20

'Maybe start with the parts that we might actually care about.' I said.

Now that Sharon's interrogation was more or less over, I wanted some real answers.

'Ah, Matt. Finally decided to join the conversation, have we?' Peter said with a tone of contempt.

'Cut the intimidation tactics Peter, or I'll start cutting you.' Sharon said with authority.

'I like this one. I was told about you, but to experience you first hand...' Peter started to say and then felt the pressure of a thousand suns pinching his shoulder blade together by Atlas' hand. 'Holy crap, that's a tight grip. Ease up there, big guy.' Peter continued.

'Maybe start talking or we can make this even more uncomfortable for you.' Sharon said.

'Fine. You win. Let's start with the Canvern. They are currently a thorn in your side, and you are a thorn in their side too.'

'Go on.' Sharon said.

'The Canvern is a ship of suspicion by Designation 13. We have suspected them of doing something outside of HSP jurisdiction or control, but we just don't have the information we need to do anything about it.' Peter cleared his throat. 'And then we hear that they are launching an all-out assault on a delivery ship, the Shadow Puppet.'

'All-out assault, huh? That sucks for us.' I said.

'It does indeed, captain Matt.' Peter stated flatly. 'This, of course, piqued our interest. I mean, what information does the Shadow Puppet have that would be of such interest to a ship we are suspicious of? It makes us suspicious about both ships.'

'That's a lot of suspicious activity.' I said as though I was telling the punchline of a joke.

Nobody laughed. I squelched my smile rather quickly. Hey, I deal with difficult things with humor.

'Anyway, rather than continue messing with the Canvern and trying to figure out what they were up to we decided it would be best to also look for the Shadow Puppet and see if they know what the Canvern is up to. Save us all a lot of time.'

'That means you want us so that you can get information on the Canvern not because the Canvern wants us dead or alive?' I asked.

Sharon shot me a look. The look that tells me that I have forgotten my place and that this is her interrogation. I bow my head and resign the questioning back to her.

'What do you want to know?' Sharon asked Peter.

'Umm, isn't it obvious from what I just said?' Peter asked like he was in a room full of morons.

'Humor me.' Sharon said as straight faced as one can get.

'I want to know what the Canvern saw that makes you the biggest target in the galaxy.' Peter said after looking around the room at everyone wondering why they don't already know the question.

Sharon thought about it. She looked at me and everyone else in the room and finally said, 'We saw the Canvern in diplomatic formation with two of our enemies. The Morps and Splims.'

Peter blinked and stared trying to make sure he just heard Sharon correctly. He looked around at us to make sure we were all in agreement with the story. How he didn't already know this being that he is Designation 13 is beyond me.

'So, you're telling me that the Canvern wasn't shooting the enemy but was in cahoots with them?' Peter asked to make sure he had it correct.

'Y...e...s.' Sharon said nice and slow, and she nodded the whole time, so that Peter could definitely make out the word.

'But that doesn't make sense. The Canvern has put the bounty on your head because they claim you have stolen highly classified materials from the HSP.' Peter exclaimed.

'Well, if that were true then you, being Designation 13, would know what it was we stole.' Sharon said. 'So, do you?'

'Do I what?' Peter asked. He was clearly in deep thought and missed Sharon's statement.

'Do you know what it is that we allegedly stole?' Sharon said slowly so that Peter could follow.

'I wish I did. But the fact that Designation 13 doesn't even know means this is big. Really big.' Peter kept looking for answers with none to be found. And finally, he begged, 'Tell me, please, what do you have that the Canvern wants so badly?'

'Listen, Pete, can I call you Pete?' Sharon started...

'No!' Pete replied.

'Pete, I'm going to go out on a limb here' Pete looked pissed that Sharon called him Pete, 'and say that we don't trust you with that information. At least not yet.'

I nodded, smiled, said, 'yeah, no, we don't.'

'This is how it's going to go. You continue to talk to us about what you know, and then we will decide what information you get in return.' Sharon said. 'Deal?'

Peter looked around the room. He definitely wasn't used to being the one with the least amount of information, and he looked defeated, deflated, and ready to throw an adult temper tantrum. 'Fine.' He finally replied.

Chapter 21

'Pete. You've given us a lot to think about.' Sharon said after Peter gave us a lot of information to digest. 'Just one thing doesn't add up. How do you know all of this information?'

'Designation 13, duh. What more do you want to know?' Peter replied.

'If what you are saying is true, then we have been fighting the wrong war for a very long time. Why has nobody stopped it?' I asked.

'Because we are winning and getting everything we want. Humans have always been the worst race in the galaxy. We use people and things to gain the advantage all the time. As long as we are gaining the advantage, why change the game?' Peter said plainly.

'Why!? Because innocent beings are caught in the crossfire! That's why! There shouldn't be any other reason!' George snapped. The rage in his eyes was unlike anything I had ever seen. He must have had some experience with something similar. I guess it might be time to sit down with George and learn a little more about his past. Sheesh.

After a few moments of everyone staring at George as he calmed himself down, we all stare back at Peter.

'Look. I gave you some of the most heavily guarded secrets in the galaxy. Will you please tell me what you have in your possession?' Peter begged.

'What makes you so sure we have anything? Maybe the Canvern just didn't like that we saw them where and when we did.' Sharon said before anyone else could say a word.

Peter threw up his hands in defeat. He sighed a big heavy sigh and said, 'Fine, don't tell me. But in the essence of showing my trust in you, you should know that you have about six minutes to get out of here and through the wormhole, before the HSP comes in and kills you all.'

'How?' Sharon asked.

'Your probe was last generation. We have monitors for jamming probes. Its response time is three milliseconds from contact to distress call.' Peter explained. 'Your probe took 2.4 seconds to hit us from the wormhole. Basically, you lost before you even knew what happened.'

'I guess I have been away from the "business" too long now.' I said. 'Melvin, to the ship fast! Get us ready to go. Atlas, make sure he gets there.'

Atlas and Melvin run out of the room.

'Everyone else, let's move.' I said. 'Sharon, do we take Peter with us?'

'No you don't.' Peter said. 'I have more information to dig up. You'll need me to do my part if you want to stay alive.'

'He's right.' Sharon said softly.

'Take this.' Peter said as he handed a small device to Sharon. 'This will allow us to contact each other when we have more information.'

'You don't seem to remember that I am ex-Bug Sweat. This is a tracking device.' Sharon said as she threw it hard against a wall.

'Can't hurt a guy for trying. Here…' Peter handed her what looked like a thick business card with a number on it. 'This will actually get you in touch with me if you need it.'

'Can I shoot him captain?' Sharon asked while pulling out her gun.

'Why? What did he do?' I asked.

'He just handed me a second tracking device after I called him out on the first one.' Sharon said holding her gun to Peter's head. 'He is now testing my patience.'

'Fine, fine, you win. That is the correct number though. If you memorize the number you can leave the "tracker" with me.' Peter said.

Sharon noted the number and broke the device in half before returning it to Peter.

'We'll be in touch.' I said to Peter as we ran from the room.

Chapter 22

'Melvin, we're in, let's move!' I shouted.

Melvin lurched us in some direction that caused me to take a face plant. Guess I should have told him we were in after putting on my seat belt.

We start towards the wormhole.

'Where do you want me to go Captain?' Melvin asked.

'Camp Adleston is the ideal spot. But I can't shake the feeling that while we were in there, someone was tagging our ship.' I said. 'So, let's put my theory to the test. Head for Mark 8.'

'Is that more code sir?' Roach asked.

'Yes Roach. It is.' I replied.

As we head for the wormhole we delete the probe. Yes, that means we make it self-destruct. It leaves very little to inspect. Not that they don't know it was us. But hey. Why make it easy on them.

Just as the probe deletes itself, we see the Canvern coming through the wormhole.

'Shit!' Melvin yells. 'It's the Canvern!!!'

'Evasive!' I yell as though Melvin didn't already know and wasn't already doing what he does.

Melvin pushes the hydrox-injector button as George demonstrated before and we start moving side to side like never before. Melvin is doing what he can to avoid the Canvern's grapple. At least long enough to get into the wormhole.

'100 meters!' Roach states over the speakers

'90 meters!'

'80 meters!'

'70 meters!'

'60 meters!'

We jar to the left which means the ship went right.

'50 meters!'

The ship spins clockwise.

'40 meters!'

We drop. How do we drop in space? I don't even want to know.

'30 meters!'

Almost there.

'20 meters!'

So close, get us there Melvin, I think to myself.

'10 meters!'

Bang! Crack! And then we all lurch forward. They got us. NO!!!

Chapter 23

I can't believe we were this close to getting away. We are certainly going to die by torture. I never really wanted to go out that way. I mean, better to be tortured by the HSP than the Splims. The Splims do experiments while their subjects are alive. And they don't kill you when their done. They just throw you in a pile with other bodies they are done with. You can't move because of the experiments and the pain is something I don't care to imagine, but you are literally left to die over time, in pain, without being able to even cry because your eyelids are missing.

Oh…wait…

'George! Do the thing!' I yelled.

George hit a new button that he installed just before we left Camp Adleston for the HSP space station. It was marked "DON'T TOUCH" just to make sure nobody did it at the wrong time.

George installed a nano shield. It is experimental tech and still isn't available to anyone. You should have seen George playing with it. It was like a kid with the first of a new toy. HE LOVED IT!!

Being rich has its perks. I get the new toys before the other kids.

The nano shield will literally cut through anything in its way. That's part of the reason it isn't available yet. To many possible safety problems. Lose some limbs, ship parts, you know, if it cuts through anything, you can imagine what might happen to anything that gets in the way like an arm or a body. There would definitely be some lawsuits.

Lucky for us, it cut through the grapple just as we expected it would. No way for the Canvern to pull the long arm back, fix what was now broken, attach a new grapple, and get back to us before we can make it the last 10 meters. We are out of harm's way again. Mark 8 is our next destination.

Chapter 24

'What or where is Mark 8 captain?' Roach asked

'Mark 8 is a who Roach.' I said. 'Her real name is Becky, but you can't call her that. She hates it.'

'It's not like I get off the ship, like ever.' Roach said sarcastically. 'I doubt I will meet her.'

I think I just fell in love with the ship. Even the ship is learning sarcasm. Yes!

'Actually, she is an engineering genius and connects with just about everyone and everything she can. You'll likely meet her as soon as we enter her system.'

'I have controls to keep people out of the ship, sir.' Roach said decisively.

'That you do. But you probably can't stop her. You'll see. I trust her though, so don't worry. She'll probably give you some unknown upgrade while she's at it.'

'She will also know if the ship has been bugged and if we are being tracked' I continued. 'Somehow she is able to block all signals in and out of the system except for those she wants to receive and those she wants to send. It's very impressive.'

'Why are we going there?'

'I like her, she owes me, and I have a gift for her.'

'Sir, you're not going to ruin things by sleeping with her. Are you?'

'Maybe someday. But not today. Today I need her help more than I need to sleep with her.'

'Should I give her access since she is just going to give herself access?'

'Definitely not. Make it a challenge. She loves it when it's difficult.'

'Will do sir.' Roach stated. 'And what should I call her when she finally breaches?'

'She goes by the name Trap. Mostly because she always has more traps waiting than you can imagine. She's never caught off guard. Or caught at all.' I said. 'She also thinks everything is a trap. And just because that isn't enough, she used to trap the bugs used for the Bugspos. Cliché, I know. But they all fit and that's what she goes by.'

'Trap it is sir. Looks like we will be exiting shortly.'

'Thanks Roach.'

Chapter 25

As expected, the moment we enter the system our ship starts doing some strange things.

'Melvin, it's best not to fight her. Just let her take flight control. She'll put us where she wants us.' I said.

'But sir!' Melvin started to protest.

'Dude. This isn't the first time you have been here. Don't tell me you don't remember almost splitting the ship in two?'

'Sir, that was the weirdest turn of events. I didn't even know the ship could operate like that. It didn't even seem possible.'

'Well, you learned something new that day. Let's not learn anything new today that could kill us all.'

'Fine.' Melvin said as he sat back in a pouting fashion.

'Roach, you still with us?' I asked.

'Yes. I'm giving her a run for her money as requested.' And then Roach's voice changed. 'And that run is over. Hello Matt. What brings you to my realm?'

It was Trap.

'Hello Trap!!! Great to hear your voice. Didn't take you long to get through.'

'Never does.' She said. 'Now talk. I know the universe is after you so coming here means you're desperate and I don't like desperate people.'

'Fair enough. First and foremost, we want to know if our ship was bugged and is being tracked.'

'It definitely is which is something that is currently pissing me off. It's only because I owe you that I am not spinning your ship around and sending you to uncharted space.'

'We figured as much and knew you could help out. That's why we are here.' I said. 'And, I have a gift for you.'

'What is it? This new nano shield I am detecting?'

'THAT'S MINE!' George shouted defensively.

'Calm down George.' Sharon and I said in unision.

'Sorry Trap. That's still going to be ours. At least for now.' I said. 'But what I do have is far more interesting. I'll tell you about it when we land. Or better yet, show you.'

'Okay. But this better be good.' Trap said reluctantly.

You may be wondering how someone who is this extraordinary at tech and protection is someone who owes someone like me a favor. Well, you guessed it, money. But not in actual payments. It's more in tech I have "smuggled" out from the corporations into her system. I figured that it would be best to have someone like her in my corner. Someone I could rely on in a pinch. So, every time I see her, I bring something of interest or value. That way she is always happy to see me, even if she will never admit it.

'See you soon.' I replied.

Chapter 26

'What'd ya bring me?' Trap said as we exited the ship and as she took her Oculose off.

Oculose. Think glasses that conform to your eyes and face to form a mask that looks like it was made specifically for you. Nano tech is amazing once you figure out how to use it. These things let you see any spectrum of light you want, with overlays of information, and pretty much whatever you want to see. And knowing Trap, her pair does way more than anyone else's in the universe.

I do think that if George and Trap went after the same goal, it would be anyone's guess as to who would finish first.

'What? No hugs?' I quipped back. Sarcastically of course. All I got was a stare that read "really?" in return.

'Don't you want to know why we are being targeted?' Sharon asked Trap.

'Not if it's gonna get me entangled in your mess.' Trap snapped back.

'Okay Trap. Calm down. Why are you so tense today?' I asked.

'Tense huh? Well, let's see. The most wanted crew to ever exist is here at my doorstep. That means I must work even harder to keep people and things out of my system. I don't like working hard.' Trap stated while staring into my eyes.

'Good to see you too, Trap. Missed your face.' I smiled. 'I don't have a gift to hand to you today but I do have something of interest that you might have an aneurism over.'

'Is it the thing Roach actually kept me from seeing on approach?' Trap asked.

'Did he actually keep something safe from your eyes?' I asked in surprise. 'Remind me to give him a raise.'

'We haven't gotten any raises.' Melvin said under his breath.

I smiled in his direction. He knew he made more than he would with any other crew. But still, the recognition would be nice for him. I guess if we survive this adventure, I'll have to do something extraordinary for the crew.

'As a matter of fact, it is what Roach kept from you.' I continued.

'I have to actually look with my own eyes and in physical form. So lame.' She said.

'That would be a starting point for sure. But I am guessing those Oculose might come in handy.' I stated.

'Let's have a look then, shall we?' She said.

I motion everyone back onto the ship and watch her as she walks by. Yup, you guessed it, to check out her ass as she went by. To my surprise…okay, not really, there she was, flipping me the bird. I think I'm in love.

Chapter 27

'I've never seen anything like it.' She said as she started putting her Oculose back on.

'Nobody has.' George said in a proud voice.

I told everyone to hold their tongues as to what it was so that she could come to the same realization we did.

As Trap explores our Pim device we all stare at her, look at each other, and back and forth for a while. None of us really know what to make of the situation. I have a smirk on my face because if anyone is going to figure this out, it's Trap.

'Is this…?' Trap started to say and then stopped. She touched her face and, just a guess, changed the spectrum of the glasses because she started looking very intently at various parts that she hadn't cared about before.

'Probably.' I said, like I knew what she was thinking.

After a few minutes of watching her she finally stepped back and took her Oculose off. She then turned to me with tears in her eyes and a smile on her face.

'It's the most beautiful thing I have ever seen.' Trap finally said.

Nobody said anything for what seemed like forever.

'I give up. What is it?' Sharon said.

'It's a Pim device. Duh.' Trap said.

'We know that much Trap. Anything you can tell us about it?' I asked.

'A bunch. But I really need to get this into my lab to know for sure.' Trap said.

'Not a good idea.' Sharon blurted out.

I'm pretty sure Sharon and Trap are jealous of one another. Or something like jealousy. Like they are both trying to be the alpha female in my life. I don't even know who would win in a fight. Sharon for sure if no gadgets were involved. Trap, if gadgets were allowed. I hope to never find out. I like them both too much to have them figure it out.

'Atlas, would you mind help getting this into her lab. And Sharon, feel free to keep it company along the way.' I felt it was time to be all captain like and start barking some orders. We do have half of the universe trying to kill us. Maybe more.

Chapter 28

In the lab, Becky, I mean Trap, started to do all kinds of scans and tests. She's so pretty. I wonder who actually gets to call her Becky. I want to be the one that gets to call her by her real name. And even then I would probably give her a playful name that only I get to call her. I wonder what it would be like to kiss her. She has such wonderful lips. She smells pretty too…

'Matt!!! HELLO!!!???' Sharon shouted as she pushed me off of my seat.

'Sorry. I was in deep thought.' I said as I collected myself.

'Sure sir. You keep telling yourself that.' Sharon said while rolling her eyes.

'What's up?' I asked.

Trap pointed to the device. 'You don't know what this is or what it does, do you?'

Shaking my head, 'Nope.' Was my only reply.

'What do you think it is?' Trap asked.

This is her game. Show you how utterly stupid you are so that she looks even better at the end when she drops the truth on you.

'A Pim device. Either the location of the Pims or a wormhole device of some kind.' I said venturing a guess.

'Maybe it is.' She said. 'You having a guess at all is closer than I thought you would be. Good job.' She said in a condescending tone.

Oh, if looks could kill, Sharon would have just cut Trap's head off.

'If it's neither of those, what is it?' I asked.

'You see this area here?' As she pointed to what could only be described as an empty tank of some kind. 'That is likely where fuel goes and it looks empty. What's even more interesting is that it looks like there is no way to refill it.'

'What does that mean?' I asked.

'It means one-time-use only, captain.' George said rather quickly.

'Look at the big brain on George!' Trap said, again in a condescending manner.

I think Sharon may actually take a swing at Trap at some point before we leave.

'Do you know who used this device?' Trap asked.

'Why?' I asked in returned.

'Well, they would know what this device did if they were the one to use it.' She said.

'We have an idea. But no proof.' I replied. 'We know that Farenx had it in their possession before us.'

'Excellent!' Trap said as she headed towards her wall of computers. 'I have direct access to everything they know.'

'Really?!?' George asked in intrigued as he started to follow her like a lost puppy.

'I'll see what I can dig up.' Trap said. 'In the meantime, make yourselves at home. You know where the food is.'

And so we do. Because until we know what this thing is, we aren't going anywhere.

Chapter 29

I must have dozed off because the alarm jarred me awake to the point where I could feel my heart through my chest.

'What's happening!?' I shout even though I don't even know who is around yet.

George and Melvin come running into the room looking panicked.

Atlas grabs at his body armor to make sure it is in place. I don't think I really ever see him take it off, now that I think about it.

Sharon enters rather calmly which actually helps me calm down myself.

'Incoming.' Trap says over the loudspeaker.

We all rush into her control room to see what is happening.

Up on the screen are about ten ships entering the system. And just as they enter, they spin around and are back on their way.

'What is happening?' Melvin asked. 'Why would they enter and then leave again?'

Trap smiles the biggest smile ever. 'It's working just as I planned.'

'What is?' Sharon asked curtly.

'I setup my system to send any ships I don't want here back into the wormhole system. And typically somewhere that will take them a month to figure out how to get back.' Trap said excitedly.

'That's a neat trick. But what about the Canvern? It doesn't seem to be turning back.' Sharon asked.

'Interesting.' Is all Trap said as she started typing away.

'Interesting? What the hell? We don't have time for interesting! Everyone to the ship!! Now!' Sharon shouted at the crew.

'Calm down everyone. They aren't getting anywhere close to here.' Trap said calmly.

'How do you know!?'

'They never have. And I keep adding new tricks to my arsenal.'

Just then, another alarm sounded. They've launched missiles!

'I supposed we aren't supposed to be worried about those?' Sharon asked.

'Nope.' Was all Trap said in return.

Just then as it seemed inevitable that the missiles were going to make it through, they turned around and headed right back to the Canvern.

The Canvern saw it coming and shot down their own missiles. Good thing they are always ready for war or it would have been fun to watch them destroy themselves.

'They're trying to actually talk to me. Isn't that cute.' Trap said with a smirk on her face.

Just then, we notice a few hundred blips on the screen. Not from the Canvern but from the planet's orbit. They are headed for the Canvern.

'What are those?' Melvin asked.

'Assists.' Trap said.

'What are Assists?' George asked with intrigue.

'They assist a ship out of my system if I can't hack their navigation.' Trap said.

And just as she explained it, they all latched on to the Canvern and started pushing it out of the system and back into the wormhole. The Canvern definitely took out a bunch of them with gun fire, but not enough to stop the onslaught.

'How did they find us? I thought you blocked all signals as soon as they come through the wormhole?' I asked.

'Must be new tech I don't know about. Some way to track ships inside the wormhole system itself. Which shouldn't be possible.' Trap said. 'Or, there is something or someone on your ship that is sharing information they shouldn't be.'

Everyone starts staring at one another, sizing each other up in an accusatory fashion. Who could it be? I can't imagine anyone on my crew who would do such a thing.

Unless…

Chapter 30

'Trap.' I said softly so nobody freaked out. 'Could you run a scan of Roach? I think he may be the traitor, but without even knowing it. Maybe his software came with a vulnerability that has been exploited by the HSP.'

'No. Couldn't be Roach.' George said, shaking his head in disbelief.

Trap started typing furiously. She has never looked worried, but this definitely put her on edge.

ALARM!!!

'Fuck!' Trap shouted, and she got up and ran out of the room.

We all stared at one another, and then almost all at once, we chased after Trap to wherever she was going.

The lights started to flicker. The screens started to shut down. Everything was going into chaos. Trap was fast. We all had a hard time keeping up. Except for Atlas, of course.

We finally catch up to her as she is entering her ship.

'Where are you going?' I demanded.

'My system has been compromised. Roach was a trojan horse. You assholes led the HSP right to me and right through my systems.' Trap said in anger. 'I'll be dammed if I am going down with the lot of you.'

'Take us with you. We need to get this device out of here and away from the HSP. We have places we can go.' I pleaded.

'Anywhere Roach has been has also been compromised. Sorry, but I don't trust you.' She said as the door started closing.

'FUCK!' I shouted.

I stared at the group, and George was in deep thought.

'George, tell me you have something. This is no time to be introspective. Talk.' I demanded.

'We might be able to disable Roach until we get things sorted out. That way we can still leave the system and survive. I don't know where we can go. That's up to you.' George said and then took off towards our ship.

BAM! And the building started to shake. They definitely launched some missiles at this place because it is beginning to fall apart.

'Atlas, Sharon, go get the device. We'll get the ship ready.' I shouted.

Atlas and Sharon took off towards the device.

I ran with George and Melvin to the ship.

'What do you need me to do?' I asked.

George just started doing his thing.

Atlas and Sharon ran in shortly thereafter. Nothing in tow.

I looked at them like I wasn't sure what I was seeing.

'She took it.' Sharon said while panting for air.

'She what?' I asked, perplexed.

'It's true. The device isn't there and we saw her ship take off just before we got back. She must have doubled back and set off a bomb to distract us.' Atlas confirmed.

'That bitch!! She must want the bounty.' Sharon grunted.

'At least she likes me enough to not ship me out with the device.' I said. 'No matter. We have Melvin and George working on the ship. We have to get it back.'

I ran into the room where George was.

'George, stop messing with Roach. It was a trick to separate us from her so she could take the device.' I shouted.

'Melvin, follow her, NOW!' I yelled loud enough for Melvin to hear in the cockpit.

'George, be ready to disable Roach anyway just in case she did what she made us think the HSP did. Remember, she's crafty and cunning. I wouldn't put it past her to put a bunch of "traps" in the way.' I said.

I turn and walk to the closest radio.

'Trap. Stop and return the device. You don't know what you are getting involved in. They will kill you. There won't be a reward. Just a bullet.'

No response. But we start lifting off, chasing after.

'Melvin…I know you're awesome but be on the lookout for some crazy unexpecting things as we leave. Her name is Trap for a reason.'

As expected, the Assists start coming after us as soon as we leave the atmosphere of Traps planet.

'Nano shields, George.' Melvin said sharply. 'That should keep them from doing anything we don't want them to.'

'How do we track her!?' I said nervously and worriedly. 'We have to know where she goes, and we have to get that device back. Peter insisted we keep it safe.'

'Not to worry captain. I never trusted that bitch. I attached a beacon on her ship as soon as we landed.' Sharon smirked. I could see she was in her zone and loving every minute of it. 'I will turn it on after we leave the system. She won't expect it at that point.'

'Sharon. I love you.' I said. But not like you think. As a friend. Calm down there. Remember, I am choosing not to sleep with crew members anymore. And besides, Atlas might crush me if I tried. That is if Sharon didn't break me in half first.

'How are the shields holding up?' I asked Melvin.

'Amazing! Can't even tell the Assists are out there. And they can't latch on. They sort of just slide right off.'

'Oooo' George said as though he just thought of something amazing. 'It's a nano shield…what if…' and he trailed off.

Next thing I see are bright lights flashing outside of the windows. I step closer, and it's actually the Assists blowing up.

'What did you do George?' I asked.

'I told the nanos to invade the Assists to muck up their internals. Causing them to explode.' George said with a smile.

'Won't that use up the nanos?' I asked.

'No sir. The nano tank is set up to cover a battlecruiser. We have a shit load to spare.' George replied.

'Great! Keep it up. Hopefully the Assists are set to return as soon as we hit the wormhole.' I said.

We see from the Vizdar output that Trap finally went through the wormhole. We are about one minute behind. That is until Trap's trap is sprung. We stop, and everyone lurches forward. But not like when Melvin uses the lateral thrusters. You see, George fixed that issue. It seems her plan of knocking us out by slamming our bodies against the walls with a sudden stop by a nano net failed. We are all still awake and ready to take on the trap.

And before I can even look for options, George is already tackling the issue.

Chapter 32

'She's good.' George said. 'But I am better.'

George sat proudly as we entered the wormhole. George was able to disable the nano net by using our own nanos against it.

'How?' I ask.

'Think of wires crossing and shorting out a system. I programmed the nanos to "mate" with the net nanos. Stick electrodes into port holes and then deliver a load that it simply can't handle.' George starts looking a little too excited. He then shakes his head and continues. 'Wait. What was I talking about again?'

'I'm sure Trap knew of that vulnerability, George, but probably didn't think anyone would know to exploit it. If anything she probably just wanted to slow us down.' I said.

'Sharon, how long until we can track her?' I asked.

'Already begun. As soon as she hit the wormhole, I began the tracking process. We'll know her location as soon as she exits.'

'Won't that make it hard to catch her before she does something stupid?'

'Not going to happen, captain.' George said, and then realized his rhyme and got a big smile on his face.

'What do you mean?' I asked.

'Remember when she said make yourselves at home?' George asked.

'Of course.'

'Well, I did. And my favorite way to feel at home is to play with ships and gadgets.'

'Makes sense.'

'I went to her ship out of curiosity, and while snooping around, Sharon asked me to put in a failsafe.' George said, motioning to Sharon. 'Like she said, "I don't trust that bitch." So, she asked that I make sure that if things went sideways, we would have the upper hand.'

'Well, shit. That's the best news we've had in days.' I said. 'Where will she end up?'

'Where do you want her to end up captain?' George asked.

'Sharon? Thoughts?' I looked over at her.

She slowly got a smile on her face remembering something that had been filed away in the old brain for later use. 'Can we please?' She asked like a kid in a candy store wanting the biggest piece of candy.

And right then, I knew what she meant. I didn't want to admit it, but she did set it up for a reason, and now we have that reason.

'Yes. You can play at Playground Appletown.'

'MELVIN!!!' Sharon shouted as she ran to Melvin's side.

The way Melvin flinched you would think he just got caught by the police for murdering someone.

Chapter 33

We exit the wormhole, and there she is, Trap, her ship stuck in the box. Mind you, it is a big box. Big enough to fit a ship into.

Sharon insisted on setting up a "Playground" when she came on board. These are areas that are set up by the HSP to disable an enemy and put them through the wringer. Make them talk, take them out of the game, or really whatever you want the playground to do. There are definitely deadly playgrounds. One wrong turn in the wormholes, and you could end up dead because of an HSP playground.

Sharon knew about these playgrounds as she has set up her fair share. She wanted one for us as a way to trap pirates if necessary. Who knew that Trap would become a pirate of sorts?

'Trap, you there?' I asked.

No response.

'Trap don't be like that. We let you live. And believe me, Sharon would like to kill you now.' I continued.

No response.

'Trap. I know you don't like being on the losing end and you're probably trying to figure out how to get out of this, but trust me, you won't. Just give us the device, and we'll set a timer on the box to let you out when we are good and gone.'

'Fine.' A soft and defeated voice finally came through.

'I thought we had something Trap. A possible future. Why would you do this to me?' I asked.

'A future? You were as good as dead if I didn't get the device away from you. Why didn't you get that when I took the device and left you planet side? I wanted you safe.' Trap blurted out. 'If I hadn't left you there, we wouldn't have a future. I only did it because I care about you.' Trap continued in a calm and caring manner.

'It's a trap sir. Don't fall for it. She's a woman. She'll use her feminine charm on you to get what she wants. For you to let her out and to gain her trust again.' Sharon said. 'Trust me on this. If she really does care, she'll wait for you when this is all over.'

I nodded. 'Hand over the device and we'll go from there.' I said trusting my XO.

She transferred the device to a box on the side of the box. It's a cargo transfer device that keeps the ship and all of the ship's signals in, while transferring a solid object through. Think of a quarantine situation where you have to pass food into a patient, and they have to provide piss back in return. But without sharing the air.

'Thanks Trap. We'll let you out when we are ready. I really hope you are sincere about caring. But I have to trust Sharon at this time and leave you here so that you don't cause us any more trouble as we do what needs to be done. We have more information than you can imagine, and this setback just makes it harder to proceed.' I pause. 'I know we are going to need your help to finish this, so please, please, please return home and get everything up and running. I'll let you know what we need and when.'

'Fuck you Matt.' Trap said, almost crying. I don't know what she means by that, but I hope she'll come through when we need her.

Chapter 34

'Now that we have the device back, where do we go?' Melvin asked.

'You mean, now that we aren't being tracked and we know it?' I corrected Melvin.

'Yeah, that.' Melvin said.

'Well, I probably need to check in with my dad to see if he has found Kip.' I said as I turned towards Sharon. 'Want to stay for this call?'

Sharon nodded. 'But I would like to remain off screen so he doesn't know I am there. I don't want to create more tension as I expect there to be a lot.'

We walk to my cabin to make the call. Atlas stops us on the way.

'Sharon. Can I have a moment?' He asks.

I leave them to it and walk into my cabin. I really want to hear their conversation, but I also know Sharon would kill me. Best to just walk away.

A few minutes later she comes into the room. Something different about her. Not sure what yet. Hmmm…

'Ready?' I asked after waiting just long enough for her to tell me what's up without it being awkward.

'Ready.' Was all I got in return. Oh well. I guess I'll find out later.

I punch in the codes to get in touch with my dad on a secure channel.

'Dad. Guess what?'

'What?' He asked in a "I don't have the time or patience to be playful" tone.

'Well, I was going to be silly but from your tone you won't be having any of that from me today.'

'Nope. Things are nuts here. Well, everywhere really.' My dad said. 'The secret is out. Everyone wants the device, they want the location, they want the power.'

My dad looked down, like he had been defeated by something. I could ask, but that might not be wise right now.

'What do you need from me?' I asked instead.

'I want you to stay safe.' He said.

'Well, once we know where Kip is, then we can get the location of the Pims, and then we can get this device away from everyone who would use it to take over everything and everyone.' I paused. 'Dad, nobody should have this device or the power that comes with it. I want to make sure nobody gets the chance.'

'I won't lie, son, I want the power just as much as everyone else. But I agree with you. It's too much for anyone to have. Even a government to have.' He exhaled softly. 'We just aren't ready as a species and our enemies definitely shouldn't have it.'

'Speaking of, do they know too?'

'If everyone here knows what's happening, then they do too. Humans aren't the only species with spies.' And there was a slight grin to his face as he said it.

'Understood. Well, then we need Kip sooner than later.'

'About that. I do know where he is but it is too dangerous for you to get him.'

'Let me worry about that.' I said in return. 'I just need to know where he is.'

After a long pause, my dad started to give me coordinates but there was a strange look on his face like he didn't do it willingly.

'And you're sure he is there?' I asked.

'He definitely is there. And you definitely shouldn't go there to get him if you know what's good for you.'

'Okay. Thanks for the advice. Better drop off before this call is traced.'

'Okay son. Stay safe. Love you.'

And our call ended.

I look over at Sharon, wide eyed.

'Trap?' She asked as in ambush, not Becky.

'Trap indeed. He didn't even say "Dad out" at the end of the call. That's how I know it isn't good.'

'I've heard my share of people saying things at gun point. Pretty sure your dad was being forced to share information that wasn't really his to share.' Sharon said.

'Explain, please.' I muttered.

'He was forced to give you those coordinates. I do believe he is telling the truth that Kip is there, but the HSP is using Kip as bait to lure you in. To capture you and the device. And kill us all, of course. No witnesses.' Sharon explained.

'Fuck.' I said with a sigh. 'Well, at least we know it is a trap. We can plan for that. But how do we get Kip out. That still has to happen.'

'We need a diversion.' Sharon said flatly. Then she got more excited, and I saw her face expand into a big smile.

'What?' I asked.

She didn't answer but she got up, smiled bigger, and ran out of the room.

I got up to follow, stared back at the screen, and said softly, 'Dad, I hope you are alright. And I'm sorry I got you involved.' And then I followed Sharon out into the hallway, down into the galley.

Chapter 35

Sharon had asked Roach to gather the crew into the galley. So, by the time I got there, she was only waiting on me.

'Nice of you to show up captain.' She said with a wink and a smile. I wasn't really that far behind. So what did she mean by that?

Doh!

I guess it took me a lot longer to recognize sarcasm after the call with my dad. I guess the situation has me thinking a bit too hard. About my dad's safety, about Kip, about humanity. It's feeling a bit heavy now.

'Captain?' she asked like I was in some sort of comatose state.

'Captain!?' she yelled.

I can hear her but am still unable to respond. What is going on in my head? I'm usually able to handle anything.

BAM!

And I'm on the floor. Sharon staring at me from above.

'What the hell was that!?' I shout.

'You needed a good smack to the head.' Sharon said bluntly and then smirked and headed back to the rest of the group.

'Okay then. That hurt. But yeah, I see your point.' And I got up to follow her over.

'As I was about to say before the captain failed at being present…'

'Hey!?'

'Get over it captain.'

'But…'

'No but's. We have a lot to do and not a lot of time to do it in.' Sharon said. 'I need your head in the game now, not in an hour or a day or however long you were planning to sulk.'

'Harsh lady. Very harsh. But yeah. You're right.' I said. 'But fuck…can you hit with less force next time?'

'We'll see.' She said. Again, with a smirk. She is really enjoying herself at the moment.

She continued. 'Here is our situation…' and she explained to the crew what we know and added in the recent call with my dad.

'Thanks to my good friend Pete,' said with a roll of the eyes, 'we know what we need to do next.'

'What?' asked Melvin and George almost simultaneously.

'Finish a war.' She said.

'Isn't the saying, start a war?' George asked.

'Typically, yes. But seeing as we have already been at war, it wouldn't be starting one, but making sure it comes to a close.' Sharon said.

'But I thought we just wanted to get this device back to the Pims.' Melvin stated.

'We do and that is the primary goal. But to get the location of the Pims, we need Kip. To get Kip we need a distraction that nobody can avoid. The only distraction that I can think of that would be big enough is a massive battle with everyone going toe to toe with each other.'

'And how do you propose we get everyone in the same place at the same time?' George asked.

'That's easy.' I said interrupting Sharon. 'We know the location of the ambush, where they want us to be. So, let's make sure everyone else knows about this location. And we can set a time that works for us.'

Sharon smiled and nodded like a proud parent.

'Does that sound about right Sharon?' I asked as though I just solved the puzzle as she was talking.

'Couldn't have said it better myself sir.' She said with a smile, and then grew a wider smile as she looked at Atlas, who also smiled back at her with pride and something else. Hmmm...what is going on with these...Oh My God!!! They finally shared their feelings with one another.

I wasn't the only one to catch on. Both Melvin and George seemed to catch it just as I did.

'Are you two?' Melvin started to ask.

'Finally together?' George finished.

'About time.' I said. 'Now. Just don't fuck it up like I did so that we don't have to find a new Sharon or a new Atlas.'

They looked at each other.

'Deal?' I asked

'Deal.' They both said in unison.

Chapter 36

'Where to first?' I asked Sharon.

'Sharon?' I repeated.

'Don't tell me it's my turn to smack you in the face to get your attention.' I jokingly said. Only to find Atlas stand immediately and in a somewhat threatening manner.

'Calm down there big guy. I'm a sarcastic ass, remember?' I reminded him.

'Sir, I know. So was my standing. I know Sharon would beat your ass if you even tried to smack her.' Atlas laughed. 'I know I don't need to protect her. That's one thing I love about her.'

'Well, now that that has been established...' I said with a big relief. And with a bit of pride that my crew is all about being sarcastic and playful. 'I believe I was asking, where to?'

Sharon came out of whatever trance she was in. I'll have to ask her what that was about; but before I could ask...

'To Morlapian space.' Sharon said. Atlas turned in surprise. My face read surprise. I'm sure of it.

'Won't they want to kill us just like everyone else?' I asked.

'Of course, but we aren't going close enough to make that happen. We are going back to Delta Tango 6118 to make a broadcast about the device.'

'A broadcast?' I ask perplexed.

'We are going to broadcast, on a frequency the Morps listen to, something about the device and where it is going to be next.'

'For what purpose. I'm missing something here, aren't I?' I asked.

'We want the Morps to show up to the coordinates you received from your dad. The coordinates that are clearly a trap. We want the Morps there to cause a distraction.' Sharon continued, 'Unless you want to try and get Kip with all of the guns pointed solely at our ship?'

'Nope. I definitely want the guns pointed somewhere other than my ship.'

'Great. Let's get a move on.'

'Shouldn't we call for backup?' I asked.

'Who did you have in mind?' Sharon asked.

'Only people I can think of are the Vants.'

'Oh, we'll contact them for backup, just not here and now.' Sharon said with a smile. 'Don't worry cap, it will all be fine.'

'Okay. I've said it before, I trust you. I'm just having a hard time understanding the moves you're making.'

'It will all make sense when the time comes.' Sharon promised.

'Okay then.' I say reluctantly. 'I'll be in my quarters.' And I left the room.

Chapter 37

As we make our way to Morlapian space, likely to be blown up immediately by the HSP or the Morps, I head back to my quarters. I just realized that I am exhausted and really haven't slept for a long time.

I figured we had some time, so I thought it best to lie down for a nap.

My mind keeps wondering how I got here. What did I do to deserve the responsibility to save the universe? What was instilled in me that I am not just turning around and giving this thing to my dad so that my family can have the advantage? Who the fuck gave me a conscience?

As I think these thoughts and many more, I can't seem to keep my eyes open, and...

ALARM!!!

'Holy fuck! What the!?' I shout out as I am jolted awake. 'Roach? What's happening?' I scream but am still in shock trying to gather myself after being in a deep sleep.

'You must get to the bridge quickly captain.' Roach replied.

'On my way, but tell me what's happening!' I demanded.

'Sir, just move quickly.' Was all I got in return.

'Fine.' And I run towards the bridge.

I'm not seeing anyone else running towards the bridge. Was I asleep so hard that the alarm took a while to wake me up?

As I approach the bridge I don't hear the usual hustle and yelling that comes with an alarm and everyone doing what they need to do to save our asses.

What is happening!?

I enter the bridge and…

'Surprise!!!' Everyone yells.

I stop and stare, eyes jetting between everyone, heart pounding through my chest, the screens, everywhere to figure out what the hell is happening. Why is this a surprise? What does that even mean?

'What the fuck is happening!?' Is all I can get out, breathless and confused.

'Sir, don't you know what today is?' George asked.

'The day we get blown up by the HSP or the Morps?'

'No you idiot.' Sharon said. 'It's your birthday!'

'And you thought blaring the alarm was a good way to start such a day?' I said in an unplayful tone. 'And to get Roach in on it?'

'Hell yeah sir!' Sharon said. 'The look on your face when you came in was priceless.'

'Fuck you all.' I replied, somewhat playfully letting out a massive sigh. 'I thought we were under attack and about to die.'

'Well, you are one day closer to death.' Melvin said. Then everyone laughed at the joke.

I laughed a little too, adrenaline finally leaving my body.

'With everything going on, why would you take the time to do this?' I asked.

The crew all looked around at each other like they were trying to decide who should answer the question. Finally they all landed on Sharon. The person who knows me the best.

'We love you. You brought us all together. We are a family. You are important to us. So we get to celebrate you. If not for you, then for us.'

I start to blush, unsure what to say. A smile forming on my face, almost about to cry. And I choose only to nod and look each person in the eyes with gratitude.

What the hell did I do to deserve such a great group of people?

Chapter 38

'Thank you all for the surprise.' I said. 'But now that I am awake and full of crazy emotions, will someone let me know the status of our new rendezvous?'

'We will be there in about an hour sir.' Melvin said. 'Sharon has been briefing us on the plan.'

'And what is the plan again?' I asked.

'Wouldn't you like it to be a surprise? Make the whole day a bunch of surprises for you?'

'Hell no! I don't like surprises. Besides, one heart attack a day is plenty.'

'Okay. Fine.' Sharon said. 'We are going to pop out, send a message to "Pete" whether he is there or not, on a frequency the Morps listen to, and then hightail it out of there.'

'What's the message?'

'It's quick and easy. We are going to tell Pete that we have the device and that it will be delivered to the coordinates we received from your dad. We are going to add a time in there so that everyone arrives at pretty much the same time.'

'What time are we choosing?'

'We need to give ourselves enough time to make sure we have all of our chess pieces in place, so, three days from now.'

'That seems like enough time. Of course, since I don't know the extent of your plan, I have no idea if it's enough.'

'It's enough sir. Without making it seem like we are playing them.' Sharon said. 'If we take too long, they will know we are up to something. Three days to get somewhere is hardly that uncommon.'

'Okay then. I guess you have this all figured out.'

As I sit back and watch everyone doing their part on the ship, I notice a quick smile from Atlas to Sharon. And she of course returns a small smirk to Atlas. Ah, young love. Hope it works out well for them. I definitely don't want to lose either of them from my crew.

Chapter 39

'Thirty seconds everyone!' Melvin shouts to the room.

'At least you gave us extra warning this time.' I said in return, then winked at Sharon.

'Is the message ready? I don't want to be here any longer than necessary.' I continued.

'Ready to go.' George replied.

'10 seconds' Melvin started to count down.

I tense up a bit, not sure about this.

'9 seconds'

I look at everyone on the ship with admiration.

'8 seconds'

I think about Sharon and Atlas and what a team they make.

'7 seconds'

I think about my dad and what he must be going through that he would set a trap for me.

'6 seconds'

But at least I know he set it for me with knowledge that it was a trap. Thank goodness for his lameness.

'5 seconds'

I guess it isn't lame anymore. Brilliant maybe.

'4 seconds'

I hope Kip is okay.

'3 seconds'

I hope we survive this.

'2 seconds'

I want to see Trap again, despite what she did to us.

'1 second'

Here we go. Let's hope this is uneventful.

Chapter 40

We exit the wormhole and before the alarms can sound long enough for anyone to realize it, we are hit!

'HOLY SHIT!!!' Melvin yells.

We start moving side to side, up and down, evasive maneuvers.

'What is happening!?' I yell

'We just got hit with a plasma cannon.' George said.

'That means…' I start to say.

'Morps!' Atlas finishes the sentence for me.

'Get to the station!' I yell.

'It's gone sir! It's not on the Vizdar. I'm only seeing large pieces of what used to be a station.' Melvin shouted.

'Shit!' I yell. 'Get us back to the wormhole!'

'Can't sir. They have it blocked off!' Melvin shouted.

I stare at Sharon. I look around. We are trapped in Morlapian space. No exit. No way back. And no HSP support. We definitely are going to die.

Bam. Hit again. Another plasma blast. This one disabled our engines.

'We're sitting ducks sir.' Melvin said. 'No maneuverability.'

'Shirt!' I screamed.

'Sir, did you just say "shirt"?' Sharon asked.

'Fuck. I guess I did. Shit is clearly what I meant to say. I'm pissed, scared, and discombobulated.'

'What do we do sir?' George asked.

'Sharon?' I deferred George's question to her.

'We hide. They will likely board us, take the device, and hopefully leave the ship until they are far enough away to blow it up. They won't spend time searching for us knowing that they will just be blowing up the ship anyway.'

'How does that help?'

'George, what can you do in the next four minutes to get the engines back online?'

'With Roach's help, I think we can be ready in 10 minutes.'

'Not fast enough. But do what you can. Everyone else, into the cargo hold panels. Hide and keep quiet.' Sharon barked.

We head for the panels.

A grapple hits the side of the ship. The nano shield seems to have little effect at defending a grapple when the shield is already on.

'I might be able to buy us more time.' George added. 'If I turn the shield off and then back on, the grapple will lose its connection, try to reattach, and then be destroyed. It will take them a bit longer to figure out how to board us.'

'Do it!' Sharon said. 'Everyone else…MOVE!!!'

Sharon looked back on her way out of the room, 'George, get hidden quick. You don't want to be out here when they board.'

I follow Sharon to the cargo bay. I hear the snap of a metal that seems to be bouncing between the nano shield and the hull. Good work George.

'Roach, remind George to hurry.' I shouted as I was moving into my hiding spot.

'Will do sir.'

I hear them coming in. They clearly broke through the shield. Didn't take them long. I guess this shield isn't all it's cracked up to be. I'll have to get George to play with it more to see if he can improve it somehow. Keep things out longer.

I hear them in the hanger. Moving around. Tossing things around.

I hear them grunting as they pick up the device.

I hear them shouting orders at each other in their native tongue.

I hear shuffling. Slamming. Crunching. Snapping.

I hear an occasional shot from their guns. Not sure what they are shooting at. I'm sure this ship is taking a lot of damage.

And I hear...

George.

No. Say it isn't so. Fuck!

He's shouting something. I can't make out the words.

Shit!

He didn't get into a hiding spot in time. They have him.

Should I jump out to save him?

No.

If Sharon isn't jumping out, what chance do I have. I need to follow her lead.

And, if Atlas isn't jumping in, I also need to hold back. He and Sharon know when to attack and when not to.

Fuck I feel helpless.

'Let me go! You got what you wanted. You don't need me.' I hear George shouting as he is being dragged out of the ship.

I hope he doesn't get tortured. I hope they don't kill him. I've let my engineer down. Why did I let us come here?

I want to call out to Roach. Find out what is happening.

I want to save George.

I want to get the device back to the Pims.

I want this all to end. But without dying.

I finally hear them leave after what feels like an eternity.

The ship draws silent.

And then I hear the popping sound of everyone coming out of hiding.

Chapter 42

'Fuck those bastards!' Sharon said as she came out her hiding spot.

I came out to join them.

'What happened?' I asked

'I don't know the full extent captain, but we need to move. Melvin! Get to the bridge and get ready to get to the wormhole. We need to get out of here before they have a chance to blow up the ship. Let's hope George finished what he needed to.' Sharon barked her orders quickly and with purpose.

'Roach, are we ready? Did you guys finish repairing the ship before George was taken?' I asked.

No response.

Why is there no response?

'Roach?!' I yelled.

'Fuck.' I muttered.

I chase everyone to the bridge. I really hope we can get clear in time.

Melvin is frantic but deliberate. Pressing buttons and doing what he needs to do.

'Atlas, get a message ready for your people. We are going to need their help.' Sharon demanded. 'Melvin! Move now! We don't have time to sit here'

'I'm trying!' Melvin shouted.

'No try. NOW!!' She shouted.

A voice in my head said to buckle in. This could get rough. I sit down to buckle in and everyone else takes the cue.

And just like last time, it was just in time. We shoot left and roll over with the force of a thousand suns. Definitely cracked a rib there.

Vizdar is blaring so many alerts it's hard to keep track. But I see the wormhole entrance ahead.

Melvin did it. We got moving just in time. And this time, there is nothing blocking our escape from this area of space.

But FUCK. They have George. How can we leave now?

How do we fix this?

How do we get the device back?

How do we get George back?

What is this going to do to our plans? Our timing?

Fuck.

Fuck.

Fuck!!!

Chapter 43

'Melvin. Head for Vant space. Now!' Sharon barked.

'Will do.' Melvin replied.

'How is that going to help?' I ask. Defeated. Sulking.

'We need them to help us go after George and the device. We know that the Vants don't care about the device. But if they know that the Morps have it, then they will want to help us get it back.' Sharon said. 'That will also allow us to get George back.'

Sharon continued. 'Atlas, let them know we are coming. We need them to be ready to go so we don't waste time.'

Sharon is so calm and clear when we are in crisis mode. Must be the years of training she had. I wish I had some of that right now.

'Captain. I need you to snap out of whatever funk you are in. You are better at this strategy thing than I am. I am shooting off of the cuff here. So, if you have any better ideas or ways to improve mine, please share. Now is the time to act, not sulk.' Sharon said to me, in my face, eye to eye, stern but caring.

'How long until we get to Vant space?' I ask.

'Thirty minutes.' Melvin said.

'Okay. I don't have anything for us yet, but I do know we need Roach online. I can at least look into why he isn't responding.' I said. 'Perhaps that will get me thinking more clearly.'

'That's a good start sir.' Sharon said. 'I will continue down the path I started. We may not need your input until we are headed back to Morp space with an army at our backs.'

'Fair enough.' I said.

'Message sent.' Atlas stated, not sounding the least bit shaken by what just happened. I wonder if he really is that calm or if he is scared too. I still haven't figured out the Vants and what their psychology is compared to ours.

I walk out of the room. Partly defeated but with purpose.

I have to get Roach online.

I have to get the device back.

And I really need to get George back. He is a friend. A good friend. A family member. Someone I care about. Someone I won't leave to torture and slaughter by the enemy.

'Okay Roach, let's get you sorted out.'

Chapter 44

I head to what could only be defined as the room where the brain of the ship is stored. In old Earthian terms, it would be the server room. But computers these days are vastly different. Much more compact and use a lot less energy. A small box the size of a child's play block is enough to run a sophisticated AI. When you have two thousand of them in a room, all wired together, it gets much more complex to solve problems.

Lucky for me. I have resources. As such, I have paid extra for the fast and reliable backup/restore package for this vast network of machines. I just have to find it.

The idea is that this device looks just like all of the other ones so that nobody hijacking the system would be the wiser.

I was given a number, two numbers actually. Row and column.

The first number was 42. Must be the column because there aren't that many rows.

The second number was 3. That has to be the row.

All I have to do is take out the cube, flip it around, hit the restore switch, and plug it back in.

And, done.

'Now what?' I mumble to myself.

The lights start to flicker. The ship shudders a bit.

'I hope I didn't screw up our trajectory.' I said to myself.

And then I hear. 'Captain, Morps are attacking the ship.' From Roach.

'Roach, you were taken offline somehow. We have already escaped the Morps. I just turned you back on from a backup that must have happened right before you were deactivated.' I replied.

'Scanning.' Was all I got in return from Roach. 'Sorry captain. I have reinitiated all of my systems. Back online. The ship is very damaged sir.'

'Yes, I know. Anything you can do to fix it up would be great.'

'I'll get the nano bots, the repair bots, and self-healing systems online and running as quickly as possible.' Roach replied. 'Where is George? Shouldn't he be fixing the ship as well?' Roach continued.

'He was taken by the Morps.'

'That is unacceptable sir. We must retrieve George.' Roach demanded.

'Roach. I didn't know you cared about George that much. I actually didn't know you could care about a human that much.' I said in confusion. 'Explain yourself.'

'Sir, George and I run this ship. Without him I feel like part of my system has been turned off or removed. It doesn't make me whole and therefore I cannot perform adequately.'

'I guess that makes sense.'

'We must go get him. Now.'

'Roach, we need to get to the Vants so that they will come with and fight off the Morps while we find George and the Pim device. The Morps took that too. Without either, the universe is in great peril.' I said. 'In the meantime, we need this ship at its best. Or as good as it can be without George.'

'Okay captain. I will work away on the ship. Just hurry. Time for an AI makes everything feel like forever.'

'It already feels like forever for me too Roach. I want him back now and having to go the other way doesn't feel good. It sucks.'

Chapter 45

'Sharon!' I shout as I run through the halls.

'Sharon! I have an idea!' I continue.

'What!?' Sharon said as I round the corner and into the bridge.

'Our plan was the bring the fight to the HSP, right?'

'Yes, that WAS my plan.'

'What if we get most of the HSP to come to Morp space and fight alongside the Vants?'

'Spread out their forces?'

'Yes, that.'

'Won't we lose track of Kip?'

'Not if they still think we are coming to them.'

'How do we convince them to send half of their forces to Morlapian space while leaving Kip partially undefended?' Sharon asked.

'Atlas.' I said.

'Atlas?' Sharon said perplexed. 'Huh?'

'Atlas will be telling the Vants that the device is with the Morps. That will get the Vants to act. We can tell the Vants they will need backup and to call in the HSP. We have also informed the Vants that the HSP wants the device for their own uses, which is bad for the Vants.'

'Yes, go on.'

'This means we need the Vants to come up with some story that will pull the HSP from their current situation into Morlapian space to help them fight, thus leaving Kip at the coordinates previously discussed because they still think we have the device and are walking into a trap.'

'So, where will we be going?'

'With the Vants, but in a different ship than the Pup.'

'Which ship?'

'The Yullion.'

'That would do the trick.'

'All I needed was a boot in the ass by you to come up with a strategy and it worked. We tell the Vants what's happening, head to Camp Adleston, switch ships, and get into the fight. Rescue George. Get the device. And then figure out how to rescue Kip.'

'Okay. Sounds good to me.' Sharon said. Then looked to Atlas, 'You have any ideas on how to get the Vants to call in the HSP without tipping them off?'

'I'll come up with something.' Atlas replied.

Chapter 46

As we come up on Vantatlian space, I start to question myself again. What if we can't pull this off? What if George dies? What if I fail and the universe as we know it changes because someone we don't want to have the device finds a way to use it and take control?

'Captain!' Melvin screamed.

'Sorry, what?' I said coming out of my own thoughts.

'We're here.'

'Ah, gotcha.' I said. 'Sharon, Atlas, I guess you two are up.'

'Atlas, are we meeting someone or just sending a message?' Sharon asked.

'Meeting at these coordinates.' Atlas said, giving the coordinates to Melvin.

'Let's go. Better to get there quickly.' Sharon said.

'Atlas, you haven't been back here since your ship was destroyed. Won't they want to debrief you?' I ask.

'Again, captain, our culture isn't like yours. We can leave for a different cause or for different reasons without issue. I chose to be with you and this crew. They will respect that choice.' Atlas said.

'Good. Cause I would hate to lose another crew member. I'm freaking out as it is.'

'I'm definitely not going anywhere, especially now.' Atlas said as he turned his attention to Sharon, who smiled in return.

I smiled too.

'Five minutes everyone. Those coordinates weren't very far from the exit.' Melvin stated.

'Okay everyone. Not sure what we need but be ready. We don't want to spend much time here. And we are to follow Atlas' lead.' I stated like everyone didn't already know. They know. They are a smart crew.

'Clearance to dock.' Melvin said.

A few loud clanks later. A bit of tension easing up because we weren't being shot at. And an exhale because we could finally be around others without the fear of getting killed. At least, I think that's what is happening.

'We're docked.' Melvin said as he stood up from his seat. 'Can I stay on the ship?'

'No.' Atlas said. 'They will find that rude.'

'I guess you better come then.' I said to Melvin with a wink.

Chapter 47

As we cross the threshold, we are greeted by four very tall Vants. They make Atlas look like an adolescent. I look over to Sharon and share a glance like I am telling her to look at the size of these guys.

She puts her hand up next to her hip telling me to calm down.

The Vant that was second from the left spoke Atlas' real name. I couldn't say it in its original form if I tried. But at least I knew that's what it was.

'...you said this was the most urgent of manners. Speak.' The Vant said. I think I will refer to him as Earl. Not sure why. Just what seems right for now.

'This must be discussed at the highest levels as it may mean the demise of our species.' Atlas replied.

'Very well. But this will be a link discussion as our Grand Irrabble is not present.' Earl said.

Grand Irrabble is like Emperor or President. The highest up in the land so to say.

'Very well.' Atlas responded.

We make our way to a link screen so we can share the knowledge with the GI.

'Speak.' Earl said as the connection was established.

'Grand Irrabble. We were in possession of a Pim wormhole device, as you are aware. We know of a trap set by the HSP to take possession of it for their own use. And in fact, it is the Farenx Corporation who ultimately is pulling the strings.' Atlas says.

'We know this. Why the recap? Get to the point.' Earl said quickly.

'The trap was known by us, and we were attempting to subvert it so we could return the device to the Pims. In the midst of our subversion, we were attacked and boarded by the Morlapians. They took our friend and the device. If they figure out the device, it could end up badly for everyone in this universe.'

Atlas took a deep breath.

'We need you to launch an assault on the Morlapians. And more so, we need you to get the HSP to help BUT without letting them know about the device.'

'What do you have in mind?' Grand Irrabble asked.

'Tell them you have intel that Delta Tango 6118 was destroyed by the Morlapians. Tell them that you had people on board. Tell them that their people and yours are being held hostage. And tell them you need their help to get to them.'

Atlas has a good plan. It might not draw a lot of ships, but it will draw some.

'If I may.' I interrupted, knowing it was really bad form.

Atlas turned around and gave me what I can only imagine was the look of death. Maybe I finally noticed something with his facial expressions. Maybe not. I didn't look long enough.

'The HSP wants us. This crew.' I said.

Atlas finished my thought as he realized what I was trying to say. 'Tell the HSP that you know several of the Shadow Puppet crew members were also taken hostage. They will ask how you know. Tell them I told you. Tell them I will be joining this mission.'

Atlas continued. 'They want the device, but they will settle for the crew. That way they can torture us.'

'Will you actually be joining us?' Earl asked.

'Not on your ships. We have a different ship with a different objective.' Atlas stated.

'Very well. We will do this for the sole purpose of getting the device back.' Grand Irrabble said.

'Once you have the device, let us know and we will order a withdrawal.' Earl stated.

'Very well.' Atlas said.

'But what about George?' I asked.

The link went down. We were then escorted to the ship. Atlas doing his best to assure me on the way without actually saying anything.

Chapter 48

'Why did it end so abruptly?' I asked Atlas as we walked back onto our ship. 'Did I ask the wrong question?'

'They got what they needed.' Atlas stated. 'George is of no concern of theirs.'

'So, they are going to attack?' I asked.

'Yes.'

'When?'

'I wouldn't be surprised if they didn't start sending ships immediately.'

'What about the HSP?'

'If they do what I asked, the HSP will likely send as many ships as possible as quickly as possible.'

'Agreed.' Sharon chimed in.

'Okay. So that means we need to get to Camp Adleston now so we can switch ships, get in, find the device, find George, and get out while the Vants and HSP are distracting the Morps.'

'Yes, we do.' Sharon said. 'Melvin. Double time it, yeah?'

'Will do!' Melvin said dashing off to the bridge.

'Atlas, explain to me why we can trust the Vants to not try and take the device for themselves? Why they want us to have it?'

'I'll do my best to explain.'

'That will be helpful, thank you.'

'The Vantatlians don't want to dominate things. They want to live in peace. It wasn't until Humans came along that we learned what war was. When the Humans clearly took control of our systems, we pleaded with them to let us be. And if they did we would forever be in their debt.' Atlas took a big breath.

'You see, the Humans saw us as massive and fierce warriors simply because of our size. They thought it would be an advantage that they could exploit when it came to fighting others. They taught us the game of war. They taught us to fight. They gave us a most horrible gift that can never be erased from our past. Some of our own expanded the knowledge that was received. We started to create our own weapons. We started creating our own style of fighting. And as the centuries passed, we lost our peaceful ways.'

Atlas looked up, closed his eyes, and continued. 'It wasn't until we had our own civil war that we were once again reminded who we truly are. A peaceful people. People who just want to be the loving and caring creatures we were made to be.'

Atlas finally stared me in the eyes and said, 'If we can end the war completely, we can go back to a life of joy and love. Back to caring for each other rather than hurting each other. That is why they will help. They know we want to return the device. They know we will. They will help us do that before they will help anyone else.'

'But how do you know they trust us?' I asked.

'Because I am the son of the Grand Irrabble.' Atlas said. 'I know what it's like to have a powerful parent. But unlike your relationship with your father, my father trusts me completely.'

I am sure I went slack jawed and was staring in disbelief because I felt Sharon pushing my mouth closed.

After I gathered myself, I say. 'Well, like attracts like I guess. Maybe that's why we ended up on the same ship.'

Atlas thought for a second, I think, I can't read his expressions. And then finally says, 'Fate is a tricky subject sir. Best not to think about it, just accept it.'

'Works for me.'

Camp Adleston. It feels like the safest place in the universe for me. Like a hidden cave that nobody knows about. For the first time in a long time, I feel like I can breathe easy. Can relax. Can…

'What the fuck!' Melvin shouted.

Crap.

'What is it?' I said as I rushed to his side.

'We have a visitor.'

'How is that possible?'

'I don't know sir. Nobody knows about this place but us. And I am sure even if George was coerced by the Morps, he doesn't actually know the route. Just that it exists.'

'Any ship signature?'

'Nothing yet, just that something came through here about five hours ago.'

'Anything else between us and the docking station?'

'Nothing I can…'

Zapppppp

We're dark. Everythings dead.

'Trap.' I said with a sigh.

'Yes, that was a trap all right.' Melvin said.

'No. It was Trap who set that trap.' I said without surprise. 'I guess she will be along shortly to take us in. FUCK!'

'She isn't scoring any points on the "desire to be with her" front, is she?'

'No, Melvin, she isn't. Best get suited up. I plan on going in, guns blazing. I'm ready to kill her.'

'Kill someone?' Sharon asked as she walked in. 'I assume you want to kill whoever disabled our ship.'

'Yup. It was Trap.'

'Yes, it seems like it was a trap. But who knows we are here.'

I roll my eyes, 'It was Trap who set the trap. Fuck, we need to give her a new nickname.'

There was some brief laughter by everyone.

'Okay. Suit up everyone. We go in guns blazing. I don't want her to have a chance. She's done.' I said in my most committed voice.

'This is Trap we are talking about, sir.' Sharon said. 'She is going to have more traps set for us.'

'Yes, but she has to come here and get us first.'

'Fair point.'

'Let's assume she has traps, move swiftly, and kill her quickly.'

'Sir, I have never seen you this angry with someone. What is happening in your head right now?' Sharon asked.

'I feel betrayed by someone I thought I could fall in love with. She turned on us for a bounty and now she has found our secret hiding spot and disabled my ship. On top of that the entire universe seems to want us dead. We carry the fate of the galaxy on our shoulders, but even that is currently lost, my dad turned on me, but at least he let me know it, my friend Kip is the missing piece of the puzzle and we can't get to him, and my friend George is probably dead or severely injured. Nothing is going our way and I want to go back to boring old shipments of stupid stuff!'

'Okay sir. Stop and breathe.' Sharon said in a slow and caring voice. 'We must stay collected or that list will get even worse.'

'We do have something going for us.' Atlas chimed in. 'The Vants are coming to the rescue. Maybe things are turning around but you don't see it yet.'

'Maybe.' I said lowering my head. 'And maybe killing Trap will make me feel even better.'

'I can certainly say that it won't.' Sharon said half laughing. 'Been there. Haunts me to this day. I don't recommend it.'

CLUNK

'I guess she is here already. That was…' I started to say and then felt our ship jerk towards the station. Must be a drone ship towing us in rather than her doing it herself. No killing her now. I'll have to wait.

Chapter 50

'Lower your weapons.' Roach said.

'Excuse me Roach? But what the fuck did you just say?' I said.

'This isn't Roach.' Roach said.

'Then this must be the bitch I'm going to kill!' I screamed.

'Way to give away our plans, sir.' Sharon said rolling her eyes.

'Oh Matt. You don't want to kill me. You want to fuck me. I know you do. But we have other matters to attend to. So, if you don't mind, lower your weapons and then we can talk like civil beings.' Trap said in Roach's voice.

'Can you at least change this dialogue to your voice? Hearing that with Roach's voice was fucking weird.' I said.

'Just put down your weapons and then we can talk face to face.' Trap said. 'And I'll be watching, especially Sharon, so don't try anything funny.

'I hate her and I love her all at the same time.' I mumbled to myself so that nobody else could hear. I really do think she's incredible. God I hate emotions. Fuck!

'Your call captain. But I don't think we have much of a choice.' Sharon said.

'Fine. Drop 'em.' I said.

'Good choice everyone. Now, come on in.' Roach, I mean Trap, said.

'You know this is my place, right?' I ask.

'I do, and I love it. Oh, and I might have made some upgrades while you were away.'

Fuck. Of course she did.

'Like what?'

'You'll see. We have a lot to discuss and not a lot of time to discuss it. I know you have a rendezvous you are trying to make, so shut your mouths and get moving.'

'How does she know…' Melvin started to ask only to be cut off by Trap.

'Because I am connected to everything. I hear all, see all, and pretty much know all. I guess you could say that I am God, but without all of the mess.'

Nope. I hate her. She has a God complex.

'But at least I use the information for good and not to destroy. I like to observe and, wow, if you knew how many people I have saved over the years.'

God complex with a conscience. I like her. My emotions are everywhere. Gah!!!

'But enough of that. We have work to do and information to give.'

I tilt my head back, look up, close my eyes, breathe out, and head out of the door. Yes, I put my head back down and opened my eyes first. I'm not an idiot. Besides, I have made that mistake before. It hurts. Not doing that again.

Chapter 51

We gather in the main room, all of us a little on edge, Trap smiling brightly.

'So.' I said, breaking the silence.

'Yes?' Trap replied.

'You said we had little time, why are you stalling?'

'I just want you all to feel comfortable before I share.'

'Start talking.' I said slowly and with a bit of hatred mixed in.

'Your plan is flawed.'

'What plan? What do you mean?'

'Your plan to lure the HSP away to fight the Morlapians.'

'How the hell do you know about that plan?'

'Because I am Trap. I have my ways. You may have gotten away but not from me. I always have backups to my backups.'

'I'm assuming there are backups to those backups as well then.'

'You're catching on.'

'And I'm assuming you found this place by hacking Roach when we came to visit.' I asked.

'Duh.' Was the only response from Trap.

'So, why is our plan flawed.' I ask, so that we can change the subject.

'The HSP isn't going to fight the Morps. They will let the Vants do that while they head for the most likely location of the Pim device. They will leave the Vants to die only to take the device. They don't care about their allies when they are this close to total control.'

'But the HSP won't know that the Morps have the device. We told the Vants to leave that out of their request for help.' I said.

'Even your dad said that spies are everywhere.' Trap said.

'You listened in on my conversation with my dad?' I asked, a little weirded out.

'I see everything, hello. Do I really have to repeat that?' Trap said with sarcasm.

'With so much airwave traffic, you focused in on me?'

'Yeah. I have a soft place in my heart for you. I thought you knew that after I literally told you that.'

'I guess, yeah, but I thought you were playing with my emotions to get the upper hand.'

'Nah. I have other ways to get the upper hand. I don't need to play with your emotions.'

I shot Sharon a "I told you so" look. She shot a "She's still toying with you" look in return. I bowed my head. Sharon won that round.

'So, the HSP knows the Morps have the device?' I asked just to make sure I was following along well enough.

'They do indeed. That is why your plan is flawed.'

'Well, shit.' I said softly.

'Except that they won't get control.'

'Huh?'

'Well, after the side track of letting you know about the spies, I was telling you that the HSP wants total control. Except that even with the device, they won't have it.' Trap reiterated. 'The device is a single use device. They might be able to figure out something with wormhole creation, but it won't be total control of the system.'

'But any manipulation of the system is too much for anyone to have.' I stated.

'Agreed.' Trap said. 'The better bet is to blow up the device.'

'Well, shit. That would have saved a lot of time. Why didn't we think of that?' I looked at Sharon.

'Because then Kip would be tortured to death for information on the Pims.' Sharon said. 'That device being in existence is the only reason he isn't dead.'

'That doesn't make sense. Why not just get the Pims location and go?' Trap said.

'Isn't it obvious?' Sharon asked.

'No.' Trap responded.

'If we went to Pim space to attack, we would be destroyed in ways we can't even imagine. They are so far advanced from us that I bet this device we are all after is like a child's toy to them.' Sharon stated clearly.

'That means they want the device to create secret entrances and exits without involving the Pims.' Trap said as though she was catching on.

'Why involve the Pims at all if it can be avoided?' I added.

'Exactly.' Sharon said.

'But then why even keep Kip alive?' I asked.

'To keep in Weavel's good graces.' Sharon said as though it was obvious. 'Kill Kip, you kill the relationship with a corporation that feeds you.'

'Makes sense. At least we have that going for us.' I said.

'Hurray.' Sharon said as flatly as possible and without enthusiasm.

'Well, at this point we still need to get the device before the HSP does. So, what do you have in mind?' I ask Trap.

'Glad you asked. Come see what wonderful things I have been doing since I have been here.' Leading everyone out of the room.

Chapter 52

'And those are just the upgrades I want you to know about. I still like to keep a few things as a surprise.' Trap said as we walk back into the main room.

'You know I don't like surprises, right?' I ask her.

'I do. But I like knowing stuff that nobody else does. So, deal with it.' Trap says as she winks with delight.

'Fine. Can we go now? George, the device, the fate of the universe, la de da, etcetera, and stuff.' Sharon asked.

I nod in agreement and we head for the ships. Yes, I said ships. The new plan requires multiple ships and multiple approaches.

'Trap, you're with Sharon. It will keep me from getting distracted. Atlas, you're with Melvin. Keep him safe.' I stated. 'I'll fly the Yullion by myself and will hopefully have George when we get out of there.'

'Seriously sir?' Sharon piped up. 'Me and her?'

'Yeah.'

'You know we will likely kill each other before we ever make it.'

'Yeah.'

'Okay, as long as you're good with it.'

'Yeah.'

'Sir. Do I need to bitch slap you in the head again? I'm pretty sure you didn't hear a word of what I just said.'

'Yeah.'

'Okay, here it comes. Don't say I didn't warn you.'

And just as Sharon was about to hit me, I jumped backwards and shouted, 'Gotcha!'

'Ugggghhh!' Sharon uttered in a frustrated tone.

'Sharon, I heard you. I trust and love you both. Do what you can to get along and figure out your differences. You two could make one of the most amazing duos in the universe if you learn to set your differences aside and stop being so defensive.' I said. 'And, if you can't, please do your best not to kill each other until after we save the universe.'

'I'll do my best....Sir.' The pause and the contempt in the word sir was concerning, but I know they will pull through and get it done.

As we walk away, I hear Trap whisper to Sharon, 'He says he loves me...' And then I couldn't make out the rest of what she said.

Dammit.

I get on the Yullion. I'm alone.

Holy shit. I'm alone.

I don't like being alone.

I'm afraid I'll never see them again.

Was this a good idea?

Did I just send us all out to our deaths?

I'm really scared. I don't like being scared.

Chapter 53

'Everyone. See you on the other side. You know your parts. Let's do this.' I radio to the others.

They all say their acknowledgements, and we are off towards the wormholes.

I can't believe I am trusting Trap with the upgrades. She could be sending us all into an ambush. She could have sabotaged the ships. She could send us all to different parts of the galaxy.

Fuck. I really didn't think this through.

'Trap, I hate to say this, but if you fucked us on this, I authorize Sharon to put a bullet through your head without hesitation.'

'No. No need to worry this time. I learned my lesson and I won't do that again. I heard what I needed to hear from the HSP and know that they wouldn't let me live even if I tried. You were right. I have to stick it to them. Because if I don't, you die. And I can't have that. I don't want that. I...'

And the communication was cut short because I entered the wormhole.

That's twice I was cut off in the middle of Trap's thoughts.

Alone, in the wormhole tunnels.

My thoughts dancing through my head even stronger than before.

I have a few hours.

Maybe I can get some sleep. Roach Y (Yullion's version of Roach) can guide the ship.

'Roach?'

'Yes captain.'

'Can you make sure we get to where we are going? I think I will try to take a nap.'

'Of course, sir.'

'Wake me if there are any issues.'

'Of course, sir.'

'Thanks buddy.'

'Of course, sir.'

This version of Roach is annoying. Apparently he isn't getting enough human interaction to upgrade himself.

I'll have to have George configure the other ships to the Pup's version of….

George. Fuck. I hope he is still alive.

I hope we find him.

I hope he isn't broken.

I hope he doesn't hate us for leaving him.

I want him back.

Chapter 54

'Captain. Wake up.'

'Huh…what?'

'It's time to wake up sir. We are approaching the rendezvous coordinates.'

'Ah. Okay. Thanks.'

I get up and walk into the galley. Start to make something to eat, then head off to the head. Forgot to pee first.

Peeing gives me time to think, which sucks because I feel like I have been thinking too much. I need to turn my brain off so I stop second guessing myself.

I head back to the galley and, yes, I washed my hands.

'Sir, you don't have time for that. We exit in forty five seconds.'

'Seriously!? You let me sleep so long that I didn't even have time to properly wake up?'

'Sir, your sleep cycle stage was at a point that it wasn't advised. But I couldn't wait any longer. I had to wake you with enough time to do the basics.'

'Fuck!' I shouted. 'Fine. Let's do this.'

I head to the bridge.

And just as I sit down, we pop out into Morlapian space.

And just before panic sets in, the Margun and the Flance popped in right behind me.

Phew. I had a mini heart attack waiting for them to show.

Yeah, now you know all the names of my ships.

Well, we are one step closer than we were. That's a good thing.

Next step is to avoid getting blown up.

As we draw closer, we can see little flashes of light off in the distance. Similar to the twinkle of the stars when you are standing planet side and the atmosphere makes the stars dance. Only instead of dancing, they blink into and out of existence. If we didn't know what was actually happening, it would be very beautiful.

We proceed ahead. Three ships. Three targets.

Trap, with her skill of obtaining endless knowledge, told me that George was being detained inside of a

Morlapian prison sphere. Think space station but for convicts. Smart really. No real way to escape without having to go into the blackness of space. No ship can attach until everyone is in their cell and accounted for. And no ship stays long enough for anyone to make it from a cell to the landing bay in time. They put the cells and the bay so far apart that by the time someone escapes, the bay can be emptied of all ships with time to spare.

How I was going to get in there, bust him out, and make it back to my ship in time, well, that's where a little bit of faith comes into play. That and a lot of gadgets created by Trap.

So yeah. Faith. Faith that she isn't sending me to a Morlapian prison to make me a prisoner.

Melvin and Atlas are headed towards the battle to keep an eye on the HSP movements. Atlas knows the Vantatlian strategies in battle. He can keep an eye on the Vants. Melvin knows ships and maneuvers.

They will stay at a good distance to observe without getting blown up. And with plenty of time to counter any attack that comes their way. Trap made sure they could stop any barrage. Of course, Trap also made them virtually invisible. We'll be keeping that tech handy for future use.

Sharon and Trap will make for the device. Trap seems to know where it is, so I will leave it to Sharon to catch any tricks Trap may pull.

As for me…here I go.

They should see me on their system screens any minute now.

And, yeah, here come the missiles.

There go my Assists. They were programmed to take all missile hits and if possible, divert the missiles back at the base. Non-essential systems only.

I draw closer to the side of the sphere where George is located.

Missiles keep coming. They keep getting destroyed or diverted.

Plasma cannons are coming soon enough.

Zappppp

'That was a weird sound.' I mutter.

I guess the new plasma condenser module Trap added to the nano-shield configuration, yeah, I don't know what the hell she meant either, seems to be working. It seems to take the plasma heat and radiation and converts it down to harmless gas that just dissipates into space.

Closer. We are getting closer. And it's getting scary because they keep sending more and more missiles and plasma bursts.

No ships though. Weird. I wonder if they were all diverted to the primary battle against the…

'Sir, incoming!' Melvin shouts over my radio.

I guess I spoke too soon. Some of the fighters broke off and started coming to the prison. After me.

I press the fancy, "In case of ships attacking" button. It readies a slew of stealth missiles. These were outlawed in the treaty with the Vants but somehow Trap figured them out and made them for, you guessed it, solving problems that save lives. My life seems to be important enough that she gave them to me.

Trap is as good at finding information as the HSP is at finding ships of interest. Well, okay, much better than the HSP.

She saw that stealth tech was in discussions and was to be taken off of the table. She wanted to make sure it happened, and the best way to do that is to find the information about stealth technology and delete it entirely from any system.

Only Trap isn't one to just get rid of useful information. She kept some of that information for herself. She had to figure out the process for making the stealth material, but that was easy enough for her.

Since she likes to be her own one-person army, she used these newly made stealth missiles to stop some conflicts before they even started. One famous example, well, famous in the fact that nobody knows the truth but they know about the event, is when a rogue Splim ship popped into a Vant territory with stolen K's. It was a suicide mission. They were going to take out the entire planet. Only it blew up before it could make it to the planet's atmosphere. I guess only a few people know the truth, and they are all in this room.

As the fighters approach, the missiles launch. One at a time. Taking each target out. Without any of them being the wiser.

We touch down.

Assists buzzing around.

Nano-shield holding.

Stealth missiles launching.

And now I hear the hull of the sphere being ripped open by hull bots programmed to destroy the hull rather than fix it.

I look at the time. I look at the number of Assists left. I look at the number of missiles left.

I sigh.

We don't have much time.

Chapter 55

I rush through the opening and head through the tunnel made by the hull bots.

It seems like I have been running forever. Finally, I find the end of the tunnel and there, on the floor, George.

Shit!

I rush over to him. He isn't moving. I can't even tell if he is breathing.

I touch his neck to check for a pulse.

He screams and pulls himself back. To the wall. In a ball. Crying. Pleading for me not to come closer.

'It's me.' I say in a soft voice. 'It's Matt.'

George slowly looks up. He blinks. He wipes his tears away. He looks at me like it can't be real.

'We have to move George. We don't have much time. Can you walk?' I ask while reaching my hand out so he can take it and stand up.

'Matt?' George mutters.

'Yes, it's me.'

'Sir? It can't be. How?'

'I'll explain later. We have to move. Time is running out.'

'Time?'

'George, just trust me. You've had a hard time here. We just need to go. Now.'

He slowly reaches his hand out to mine. I grab it. I pull him up. We start moving back towards the ship.

Slower than I want us to be going, but still making progress, I can hear an alarm. That can't be good.

'George, can you walk faster. We really have to get moving.'

'I'll try.'

And we do. We move a little faster.

We make it to the ship. I sit George down in the nearest seat and run for the bridge. As I'm running, I shout, 'Roach, seal the hull and get us out of here.'

'Will do captain.'

As I reach the bridge, I see what the alarm is about. We don't have any more missiles. But we do have incoming fighters.

Three fighters coming super close. Weapons range in about 10 seconds. And we still have to wait for the hull to seal up. It's going to be close.

Just as the time got to 0, the three ships exploded into large balls of fire.

I don't know what destroyed those ships, and I don't have time to care. The hull is sealed, and we are headed back to the wormhole.

The plan was for each crew to do their part and head back once they finished. Melvin and Atlas will be able to see us leave, and they will bring up the rear once everyone is out.

And we are clear. Back to Camp Adleston.

Chapter 56

Did I mention I hate waiting? Well, I hate waiting.
I've been back for what seems like hours. Still no
sign of either ship. At least I'm not alone.

I guess now is as good a time as any to tell you that
time-shifts happen in the wormhole system.
Fortunately for humanity, it is minutes or hours rather
than days, months, or years. If time-shifts occurred
with huge variation, we would never use them
because we could come back and everyone we know
would be dead.

These shifts usually occur when there is a lot of
traffic at an entrance. I wonder what caused this one.

Of course, George isn't saying much. He can't really.
He is in a MedPod. Yeah, probably what you guessed
it is. A sealed pod where you put sick or hurt people.
It does things to make you better. I've only ever been
unconscious in one, so I couldn't tell you what
actually happens inside. Maybe that's by design. Oh
well. At least I know George is back. And other than

psychological damage, he should be fine in no time. Physically at least.

Waiting sucks.

The station version of Roach chimed in, 'Movement at the wormhole captain.'

'About time.' I say as I run off to a screen to see what's happening. 'I only see one ship.'

Come on. Please. Melvin can't be far behind. Please.

After what seemed like forever, another ship appeared on the screen. It's slower than it should be, but it's Melvin and Atlas. I hope they are okay.

I head to the docking bay to make sure everything is ready for them to arrive.

I get the repair bots on standby, ready to help Melvin's ship. Sharon's too if necessary.

And now I am waiting. Did I mention that this rock is currently four hours from the wormhole? Fuck. It's too far. Why do things have to move in space!?

I hate waiting.

I walk back to the MedPod to check on George. The system still says approximately four hours.

Well, I guess everyone will be here around the same time. And nothing to do until then.

I start to wander around aimlessly. Feeling helpless. I need something to do. I need to keep my mind occupied.

I need…

Alarm!

'Another ship entered after the Margun.' Roach stated. 'They will overtake the Margun in five minutes.'

'The hell they will!' I said with determination.

I head to the control room. Trap showed me the improvements she made, and I was only half paying attention because I never thought they would be needed. It seems like she knew something I didn't.

I think THIS is what I am looking for. 'Roach, if you know differently, let me know now.'

'That's definitely going to help sir. I highly recommend pressing that button now so that the Margun can arrive safely.'

'Glad someone was paying attention to Trap when she was explaining things.' I mumble to myself in an accusatory tone. Yes. I am currently blaming myself for yet another stupid thing.

I press the button. All that I can see is that the screen shows one less ship than before. And luckily, it was the one farthest away.

'What did that button do Roach?' I asked now that I could take a breath.

'It activated a nano-shield with wrapping self-destruct.'

'You mean…?'

'Yes, the shield wraps around a ship and then self-destructs. And, in doing so, destroys the ship caught in the net.'

'How did it know which ship to attack?'

'Trap programmed the system to attack any ship that wasn't one of the five on this station. As well as her ship or any ship with the correct deactivate code. Which is likely to only be one that Trap is in control of.'

'Makes sense.' I said, half paying attention again. 'I guess it's back to the waiting game. And maybe a nap. I have the time whether I want to admit it or not.'

'I'll wake you with time to spare sir.'

'Thanks Roach. I guess the ship and you discussed what happened last time.'

'That is affirmative sir.'

Chapter 57

'Sir, it's time to wake up.'

I am shocked I could actually take a nap. I must have really needed it. I checked the screen and the MedPod. I still had thirty minutes to get ready. Time to eat and maybe get in a shower. I don't remember the last time I had one of those. I'm sure I'll get flack for it, but hey, I don't mind.

I head for the shower, and just as I'm getting in, I hear a grunt from the other room.

'Who's there?' I shout.

More grunts and the sound of shuffling.

'George!?' I shout again. 'Is that you?'

'Uhghgh' Is all I can hear, and even that I can barely make out.

I throw on some clothes and head towards the noise. No shower for me today.

'George, dude, sit down. What are you doing out of the MedPod so soon?'

'Am I?'

'Yeah, it said there was thirty minutes left and now here you are only five minutes later.'

'I dunno.'

'How do you feel?'

'Okay, I guess. What day is it? How long have I been gone? Where is everyone?'

It seems George is coming back to life and starting to become more aware of his surroundings.

'Well, you've been gone for only a couple of days.' I didn't want to use the word hostage or captive. I don't want to set him off in a bad way.

'The things…' and George trailed off.

'The things they did…' and George started to weep.

'It's okay. You don't need to talk about it yet. Just breath. You're safe.' I say while ever so gently touching his shoulder, hoping a gentle touch would be okay.

George winced but then relaxed. 'I…but…they…the things…'

'George. Breath, please. Just relax. You've been in a MedPod for hours. Collect yourself and your thoughts. No need to strain yourself. The rest of the crew will be back in a few minutes. We can just sit here and be in silence. Take the time you need.'

George looked up at me with tears in his eyes. He didn't need to say it. I knew what he was thinking. It was a thank you and it was a plea for help. It was helplessness and hope all in one. I just offered a hug. He took it. We sat there for a long time. George cried. I held the space for this man to let it all go. To start the healing process. I probably needed that hug just as much as he did.

Please let the rest of the crew be safe and healthy. I don't think I could stand seeing another member of this crew injured, captured, or dead. I don't think I could take it. Not one bit of it.

Chapter 58

'The Flance has docked sir.'

'Thanks Roach.' I looked at George. 'I've got to go to the docking station and check on Sharon and Trap. You want to come with or stay here?'

'I'll…Trap?...But…' George looked around. Lost. Unsure of himself and his surroundings.

'Come with me George. Best to be around people than alone. Alone will allow the voices to creep up on you when you least expect it.'

'Okay.' George said, bowing his head, and shuffling towards the dock.

I walk slowly with George so he doesn't feel left behind. I never want to leave him behind again.

We make it to the dock, and out come Sharon and Trap. Nothing else.

'George!' Sharon shouts and runs towards George.

George winces.

Sharon sees it, slows down, and gives George a big yet gentle hug. I didn't know Sharon could be loving in this way. But hey, whatever. George needs all the love we can give him.

Trap seems relieved to see George and I in relatively good order.

'Glad to see you guys made it back without killing each other.' I say to Trap and Sharon.

'Well, the day isn't over yet.' Sharon said.

'You got that right.' Trap said.

Wait, are they getting along? This doesn't seem like contempt but rather playful banter.

Trap heads over to George. George and Trap look at each other. Trap doesn't say anything and George doesn't say anything either. They share a gaze of appreciation. The kind of gaze where they know that they are equals and they are glad to see each other. Trap admitting she and George have a lot to learn from one another; George a realization that without Trap, he wouldn't be free from the Morps. All from a single look. And a slight nod at the end.

I look back and forth between the two of them, 'So, where's the device?'

'Funny story.' Trap says.

'Yes, it is.' Sharon said in agreement.

Chapter 59

'Well, where shall I begin?' Sharon asked.

'After takeoff. Plus it will be easier for me if you tell the story. And feel free to share all of the juicy details.' Trap said.

'Good idea. I like seeing you blush.'

Sharon began her story…

As they took off Sharon immediately confronted Trap. 'If you are leading us into a trap I will kill you before the trap can be sprung.'

'We really should change my name. I get confused when people are talking about traps or if they are talking about me.'

'Yes, we have discussed the same thing.'

'Anyway. Don't worry about it. Like I said, I care about Matt and won't be doing anything stupid again. I want Matt to win. It's the only way we can be together.'

'You're not good for him.'

'Oh really?'

'You manipulate. You demand. You subvert. Yet you never actually show empathy, compassion, or even a romantic interest in the man.' Sharon stated. 'In fact, I don't think I have ever seen you two hug or touch outside of a handshake.'

'Well…' Trap began to say but then stopped.

'Well, what?'

'It's…'

'Spill it bitch!'

'It's just that I am not good with emotions. My parents weren't around much. I didn't have many friends. I really had to just fend for myself. I certainly have been in relationships, but they were abusive. They weren't loving or caring. I always had my guard up. Matt seems different. He really does. I just don't know "how to be" around someone like Matt. Someone who cares. Someone with compassion. Someone who wants more than just sex.' Trap said with tears forming in her eyes. Then quickly snapped out of it. 'And don't call me a bitch.'

'Consider for a second that you do decide to explore a relationship with Matt. Assuming he doesn't want to still kill you. If you don't figure it out, I will make your life miserable if you hurt him.'

Trap stares at Sharon for a few moments. Then asks, 'Wait. Do you love Matt in that way too?'

'What!?' Sharon said with surprise. 'Hell no! I am in love with Atlas. Matt is more like a brother or a really good friend. Someone I could share my deepest secrets and not feel judged. There are so few people in this galaxy that are like him that I will do anything to protect him.'

'Oh.' Trap said with a bit of remorse. 'And here I was thinking we were in competition for his love and affection.'

'And here I was thinking you were out to hurt him. On purpose.'

'No. Definitely not. I could see myself settling down with Matt.'

'Well. I'm glad we got that figured out. This should make for a much easier trip.'

'Incoming message from Matt.' Roach said.

'Trap, I hate to say this, but if you fucked us on this, I authorize Sharon to put a bullet through your head without hesitation.'

'No. No need to worry this time. I learned my lesson and I won't do that again. I heard what I needed to hear from the HSP and know that they wouldn't let me live even if I tried. You were right. I have to stick it to them. Because if I don't, you die. And I can't have that. I don't want that. I... love you. I want us to be together.'

'Sorry Trap. The transmission was cut off just before you said the word Love' Roach said.

'Dammit!' Trap said. 'That was hard for me to say.'

'It's okay Trap. You'll get your chance.' Sharon said, patting her on the back.

'I hope so.' Trap said while looking down at her feet ever so slightly defeated.

Chapter 60

'Here we go!' Sharon said as they entered the system. 'Our location is set on auto pilot.'

'Perfect!' Trap responded.

'Let's get suited up.'

'You handle the people, I'll handle the systems.' Trap said with a wink.

The two of them gear up and get ready to dock.

ALARM!!!

'As expected, they are launching missiles.' Trap said.

'Gotcha, launching counter measures.' Sharon replied. 'Let's see what these Assists can do.'

'It should be a glorious show. Unfortunately, we need to concentrate on our goal.'

They get closer to the Morp home world. Intel said that the device is stored in their most secure location on the planet. How the two of them were to get in and out without dying, that's a feat only a genius and a warrior could tackle together.

'Global defense systems engaged.' Roach stated.

'Run program "Up Your Butt Bitches" Roach.' Trap said with joy in her voice.

Roach ran the program and all of the defense systems turned on each other. Blowing themselves out of orbit and into oblivion.

'So, you could have ended this whole war years ago by telling the HSP that you could destroy their defense systems?' Sharon asked.

'I could have. But that would mean a lot of Morps dying. I want the war to end, but not through genocide.' Trap said.

'Fair enough.' Sharon said.

The ship continued into the atmosphere and landed right on top of the Galamose. The most secure building within the perimeter of what would be considered the Morlapian government.

'I'm surprised we aren't being shot at by just about everything.' Sharon said as though she was expecting to be blown up at any minute.

'Well, the program is still running. They can't even see us at the moment unless they walk outside. And at this time of day, they definitely won't be doing that.'

The Morp home world isn't that nice of a place. That is probably why they want to take over other planets.

They can really only come out at dusk and dawn. Otherwise, it is too cold or too hot.

'Ready?' Trap asked.

'Ready.' Sharon replied.

'Let's go shopping.'

They leave the ship and Trap throws down a big rectangle on the ground. Seconds later the roof inside of the rectangle disintegrates. The nanos in the rectangle each grab and pull little segments of the roof, and when you have thousands of little things tugging in different directions all at once, well, it doesn't take much for things to fall apart.

Sharon leaps inside and before she hits the ground, she shoots off two rounds. Each deadly accurate. Each causing a Morp their life.

Sharon whips around looking for more targets, looks up, and nods her head to let Trap know all is clear.

Trap drops down.

Trap pulls up a schematic of the place on her Oculose. 'This way.' Trap said.

They proceed down various hallways, Sharon dropping Morlapian soldiers as they go.

Trap springing traps, opening doors, disintegrating walls, and moving through obstacles like butter.

They get to the main research area where the device is being kept. Trap stops Sharon. 'There are thirty soldiers standing guard, and I'm sure they know we are coming. On top of that, there are sentry turrets ready to fire at anything moving.'

'I am guessing you have a plan?' Sharon asks.

'Of course!' Trap said with a smile.

Trap went into Oculose mode, where it appears she shuts down at being a human and enters a digital realm that only she can understand.

Shortly after that, the sentry turrets start letting loose. The loudest sounds Sharon had ever heard. These turrets weren't just normal turrets; they were plasma cannons.

'I've only ever experienced those in space where there is no sound. This is insane!' Sharon shouted as Trap continued her magical work.

After a few moments. Silence.

Trap lifted her Oculose and Sharon looked at her with a disappointed look.

'I thought you were going to leave dropping soldiers to me?' Sharon said with a bit of sarcasm.

'I didn't want you having all of the fun.' Trap said with a wink and smile.

They slip around the corner and see the device. Trap said, 'Cover me while I secure the device.'

'How are you going to lift it?'

'Nanos. Duh.'

'Of course you are. You love those things.'

'Hell yeah. They are so versatile.'

'Well, hurry up. I'm guessing we have moments after that loud exchange of massive death.'

'No need to worry too much. I have the turrets set to fire at anything non-human.'

'Won't that shoot at the device then?'

'No. Just Morlapians. Sorry. I should have specified that.'

'No worries. As long as we can get out of here.'

'And here we go.' Trap said.

The device rolled along the floor at a pretty slow pace.

'Can't you speed that up?' Sharon asked.

'Umm, well, these nanos are smaller than the human eye can detect. So, they are moving at the equivalent of 200 kilometers per hour if we were doing the same thing.'

'Oh.' Was all Sharon could say with a slight expression of being impressed.

They continued forward and got back to the ship with little resistance. Seems like between the attack and the turrets, which did go off a few times, the Morps kind of gave up on the device.

'It seems Matt was right. We do make a good team.' Sharon said as they re-entered the ship.

'Agreed. Let's close up and get out of here.' Trap said.

'One second.' Sharon said. And then proceeded to drop a small device into the roof opening.

'What was that?' Trap asked.

'A parting gift.' Sharon said with a smile.

'How much time do we have?' Trap asked.

'Better to get out of here sooner than later.'

'Oh shit! If it's what I think it is…'

'Yup.'

'Roach! Let's move!' Trap shouted.

Chapter 61

The ship takes off, headed to space. Just as they reached the edge of the atmosphere, the entire Galamose disappeared into a brilliant ball of light. The surrounding buildings seemed to move sideways in a circular dispersion.

'Was that?' Trap began to ask.

'Yes, it was the warhead of a K.'

'But…that wasn't the plan.' Trap said with concern.

'I know. Think of it as retribution to all of my comrades I lost during my time in service. I can't tell you how many missions we launched to get that close to their central command. Only to have them fail.' Sharon paused, tears in her eyes thinking of all of the people she knew on those missions. All of the people lost. 'I needed that closure. My fallen comrades needed that closure. They deserved to not die in vain.'

'I can't say I fully understand. I've never been in the service. But I do know about revenge. It might be the closest I can get to understanding.'

'It's a bit deeper than revenge, but yeah. You could say it stems from revenge.'

And they sat in silence as they continued towards the wormhole.

'And that's about it to our little adventure.' Sharon finally said.

I walk up to Trap and look her in the eyes. 'Did you really mean those things you said about you, me, us?'

It took her a few seconds to say anything, 'Yes.'

I take her face in my hands, look her in the eyes, and then lean in for the kiss. Her face lunges into mine as she reaches me faster than I expected. And there we were, in front of everyone, making out like we were catching our breath for the first time.

'Wow. Excuse us, you two.' Sharon said.

I pulled away, looking at her face with a big smile.

'Umm, sorry. Back to your story, maybe I'm missing the punchline, but why was it a funny story?' I asked.

'Dude. Really?' Sharon said 'You didn't catch that part at the beginning? The misunderstanding that Trap and I had about each other?'

'I caught it. But why is that funny?'

'Cause now we are like sisters, and I never thought that would happen. So, now I have to tell both of you, don't fuck it up. I would hate to have to choose.'

'Okay, so, funny to you two. Don't fuck it up. Got it.'

'Don't fuck it up.' Trap said in agreement.

'Anyway.' Sharon rolled her eyes, 'Where is the Margun?' Sharon asked. 'They weren't far behind when we left the Morp system.'

'They were limping back when some ship entered behind them. I used some of your new tricks Trap and it worked. But I am guessing it will be several additional hours for them to make it back unless we meet them and tow them back.' I said.

'Roach. Send the Rock.' Trap said.

'Affirmative.' Roach replied.

'The Rock?' I asked.

'It looks like an asteroid but it is an oversized Assist. It will push them back faster than they normally would.' Trap explained.

'Cool.' I said. 'Well, everyone, take a few to get changed, cleaned up, and get some food. I'm sure we'll have another good story to hear from Melvin and Atlas when they return.'

'Speaking of, have you received any calls from them? Seems odd that they are limping back and not calling for help.' George asked very quietly.

'Don't worry too much George. We are jamming communications so that nobody finds this place. Of course, the fact that someone followed them here is a little weird. Let's just hope it was a fluke.'

'But they do have LOSComm. Shouldn't that work here?' George asked.

'Good point. Roach, are you receiving anything from their Line Of Sight Communicator?'

'Nothing sir. I'll send a request for info.'

We wait a few moments.

'Nothing sir.'

'Okay. Well. There is nothing we can do for now. We'll just keep an eye on them and wait for their return. In the meantime, George, head to the galley and relax. You've been through a lot.'

The Margun finally made it back and Roach let us know it was time to make our way to the dock.

We head to the dock. We all have smiles on our faces. We seem like a relaxed bunch. You wouldn't think the weight of the universe was on our backs. Things finally seemed to be going our way.

The doors start to open and our smiles start to fade as the vision of Melvin dripping with blood being carried by a limping Atlas was nothing to smile about.

'Move!' Atlas demanded as he made his way to a MedPod.

We all move. I follow Atlas. Sharon shortly thereafter. Everyone else following closely behind Sharon.

'What happened!?' I demanded.

Atlas just continued to the pod and placed Melvin inside. He punched a few buttons.

'Lay off captain.' Sharon snapped. 'Atlas, you get in the other MedPod now.

'I'll be fine.' Atlas said softly.

'The hell you will. I want you in the pod. Now. I want you healthy.' Sharon said bluntly.

Atlas didn't say anything but instead, put his arms around Sharon and gave her a big hug. Holding her close and with a gentle grip.

'We were attacked out of nowhere, and our defensive systems wouldn't engage.' Atlas said.

'But how?' Trap asked as though it wasn't possible. That what Atlas said couldn't be true. 'How did they attack without you seeing them coming?'

'Stealth?' Atlas said with a shrug.

'Stealth?' I asked. 'But that doesn't make any sense. I know Trap figured it out, but I know it was outlawed by the HSP.'

'Don't be so naive captain.' Sharon said sharply. 'The HSP never intended to actually get rid of that tech. They simply hid it from view. It is used only if absolutely necessary. Because if it was found out that it was being used, the treaty would fall.'

'But…' I started to challenge what Sharon was saying, but I knew deep in my heart that the HSP would never take away options for superiority in the stars. And I bow my head, knowing the truth.

'I guess I wasn't as good as I thought about deleting the specs on stealth. They must have had a backup I didn't know about or couldn't find.' Trap mumbles in the background, low enough that nobody hears her.

'Fortunately, Melvin saw the missile before it was too late. And thanks to George...' Atlas nods to George. 'We moved sideways so quickly that the missile went right by. By the time the missile turned around, we were dodging missiles like we were in an asteroid field where all of the asteroids were blowing up, and fragments were flying everywhere.'

Atlas continued with the story...

Atlas and Melvin saw the Yullion headed for the sphere prison, and as was their task, they watched the ships off in the distance. Atlas assumed that when they called Matt to tell him that some ships had broken off and were headed his way, that is when the stealth ship locked onto their target. The Margun.

The two of them continue to watch the action. They saw the Yullion leave the sphere heading back to the wormhole.

'Looks like the captain's mission was a success.' Melvin said.

'Looks like Trap's defensive systems helped him from getting destroyed. There's hope for us if we should be attacked.' Atlas responded.

'Where's the Flance?' Melvin asked.

'Looks like they are still on planet.' Atlas said. 'A good hour away if they leave now.'

'They need to hurry. The whole battle is getting closer, and the Morps sure noticed their defense systems going down.'

'Agreed.'

They watched and waited. And as the Flance finally took off, they saw a brigade of ships breaking off of the fight and heading toward Sharon and Trap.

'We have to stop them.' Atlas demanded.

'And yet Sharon said not to. She said that their defense systems would keep them safe.' Melvin said sheepishly as though reminding Atlas would cause Atlas to punch a hole through him.

'Yes. That is what she said.'

And just as the Flance went by, the stealth ship did its business. Before the missile was launched, something took our defenses offline. Without us even knowing.

'A Door Knocker.' Trap said. 'It's a device I created once and was stolen by the HSP. It was before I learned to have backups to my backups to my backups.'

'You created the Door Knocker?' Sharon asked in surprise. 'Why, that was my favorite tool of the trade.

Gave us a lot of success in some of our really covert missions.'

'Yeah. That was me.' Trap said with pride and shame all in one. 'And that's also how they tracked you back to this system. I'll go make sure it isn't sending a signal anymore. But that also means we need to leave this system as soon as possible.'

'Well, fuck. There goes my favorite hiding spot.' I said.

'Sorry.' Trap said and I truly believe she meant it.

'Anyway…back to the story there Atlas.' I said.

'Well, the Flance made it back to the wormhole.' Atlas said. 'We sent a message to the Vants telling them the mission was successful so that they could retreat.'

Atlas then bowed his head.

'Shortly after the Flance went through and as we were departing the system, a fleet of Splim Vayps came through the wormhole.'

'That explains the time-shift and why it took so long for you to return.' I said, interrupting the story.

Atlas continued. 'Between the Splims, the stealth ship, the massive amount of missiles, well, it was only because Melvin is so good at flying that we were able to survive the attacks. We were hit badly and took a massive blow just before entering the wormhole. It knocked us both out and threw us both across the ship. Melvin must have hit every console and beam from one end of the ship to the other.' Atlas bowed his head. 'I'm sorry captain. I failed you. Please forgive me.'

Atlas kneeled as a sign of respect. And knowing that he was limping before means he kneeled despite the pain it was clearly causing.

'No. Atlas. You didn't fail. Melvin is here. He is alive. Be it barely. But the MedPod will fix him up in no time.' I helped Atlas stand back up with Sharon taking Atlas' other arm to help.

'Rest Atlas. You deserve it.' I added. 'It's not every day that someone survives an attack from a stealth ship or the Splims. You are double lucky today.'

'I just hope the Vants made it out of the system without much damage. I'm sure the Splims showed up to take out as many Vants as possible. I really hate that they are angry with the wrong species.' Atlas said with confusion, anger, and sadness all at once.

'One more question, does anyone know what took out the Morlapian fighters as I was escaping?' I ask.

'From what we observed, it was the global defense system turning on their own fighters.' Atlas answered.

'Sweet!' Trap said with excitement as she reentered the room. 'It worked better than I thought it would.'

Chapter 63

'Trap.' I said, facing away from her, then turning to look her in the eyes. 'Tell me that the Margun has some record of the stealth ship being a real thing. We may need that information for leverage.'

'I'll check.' Trap said and dashed off into the ship.

'Everyone not currently being treated for something. We need to pack up and get ready to leave. We may have to self-destruct this place and the Morgun unless Roach and Trap can get it working quickly.' I said. 'We don't know how much time we have but just because we stopped the signal doesn't mean they don't know where this place is.'

I turned to George and looked him in the eye. 'George. Are you good? Can you help?'

'Captain. If you don't mind, I'd like to stay here with Melvin for a while.'

'Take all the time you need.' I said as I darted off to do what I could.

I quickly look back as I'm leaving the room.

Have I been oblivious to the connection that George and Melvin share? Is it possible that they don't just act like brothers because they are on the ship together? Maybe they are brothers. Or an old couple? What the hell is their relationship?

I don't have time to figure it out. I need to get things ready for a quick departure.

Sharon, Trap and I are the only ones who can really do things at the moment. Atlas will probably skip the pod and help out as well, but I hope he actually heals. We may need him at full strength soon and I would rather he heal now when nothing is attacking.

'Leave the food and everyday items. We can replace those. The weapons and tech, get those installed, latched on, stowed, whatever. They can't be left behind.' I shouted as I ran around frantically.

Trap appeared from the door of the Margun.

'What's up?' I ask.

'The ship is toast. We can't fly out of here with it. We'll have to delete it when we leave.'

'Bummer.'

'Yeah.'

'What about the evidence.'

'Nothing usable. Just our eyewitness testimony. And that won't hold up in any court.'

'Fuck. Oh well. Get it ready for deletion.'

'Already done.'

'Great. Help us get the other ships loaded up with our weapons and tech.'

'We will take the remaining four ships and your ship if it is still around and head to Tuck Tuck's Tomb.' I said. 'We will autopilot all of them except the Pup. I won't separate the crew again. I can't handle it. I almost went nuts on my own.'

'Okay. For once, I am feeling very lost. Tuck Tuck's Tomb?' Trap said with confusion. 'I know pretty much everything but have never heard of that thing, or place, or whatever it is.'

'Good.' I said with a smile and a wink.

Chapter 64

I head back to the MedPod and check on George and Melvin.

'How's it looking George?'

'Not much longer sir.'

'I'm afraid we might not have enough time to let him finish. It has been hours, and every minute is another minute that the HSP gets closer to us.'

'Understood sir.'

'George.' I say, holding on to his shoulder. 'Melvin will be okay. The MedPod hasn't provided anything but status updates. He is out of the woods on anything major. Now it's likely just cuts and bruises.'

'I know sir. I just feel like I haven't seen him in days.'

'You haven't.' I say. 'Hey, if you don't mind me asking, what is it with you two? I mean, you fight like brothers. You sit here like a lover not wanting to leave the side of their partner. I just haven't figured it out.'

George looks up at me. He looks down. He looks at the pod.

'Well, sir. Melvin and I go way back. Way before either of us knew about you or the Pup.'

'Really?'

'Yeah. We were in a boarding school together. Our respective parents really didn't want us around and shipped us off for someone else to deal with us during the school year.' George took a breath. I could tell this next part was going to be hard for him.

George continued, 'The boarding school wasn't a good one. It was the one our parents could afford. That means the staff wasn't the best either. And that means we were beaten, yelled at, forced to do manual labor, and threatened that if we told our parents about it they would break our legs.'

'That's awful.'

'Melvin and I had each other's backs. We looked out for each other. We, together, took the school down. Literally.'

'Wait? Are you talking about Marble Corner Boarding School?' I asked. 'That was big news! I thought it was taken out by the Morps through some surprise attack that the HSP has never been able to figure out.'

'Then our plan worked. Because that's what we wanted it to look like. I was young, but I knew mechanics and tech. Melvin was young, but he knew flight maneuvers and flight systems.' George said. 'Yes. We were a couple of nerds.'

'Wow!' I said with a bit of pride in my voice.

'So, one day, after being beaten for not finishing our lunch, which was disgusting by the way, we decided we had had enough. We snuck around and found the parts we needed to build a drone. One that looked like and would be found as a Morlapian device. I built the systems and the weapon that would shake the campus to the ground.'

'And?'

'Once we were ready, we did our best to warn the other students, but we also knew that it would raise suspicion. We gambled and hoped that the school had safeguards to keep everyone safe from an attack. Pretty standard at most schools. But as we found out when we launched, the school cut back on anything involving safety, and as a result, almost every single innocent student we were trying to protect and save…died.' George lowered his head. He started crying.

I didn't say anything. Just put my hand on his shoulder.

'I've never admitted it to anyone before.' George said after collecting himself. 'I didn't realize how much guilt I put on myself.'

'I can only imagine.' I said not knowing what else to say.

'When Melvin and I realized what we had done, we swore we would keep it a secret and would go our own ways. We decided we would never let anyone know that we knew each other. We didn't want them putting the pieces together. We didn't want anyone knowing we were involved.'

'That makes sense. I don't blame you for doing what you did or how you moved on.'

'When I came on board, I thought I recognized Melvin but wasn't sure of it. He had the same thought about me. Once we figured it out, we decided to keep up appearances and not tell anyone that we knew each other in a previous life.'

'But you were brothers. Surviving the same storm. With regret and guilt nipping at you. You bicker with one another because you haven't been able to heal from what happened when you were kids.' I surmised.

'Yes. That sums it up. Neither of us wants to admit our horrible mistake so we push each other because we have nobody else to blame. We make each other suffer because...'

'Stop. George. It's in the past. You can let it go. You were kids. You were being hurt. You made a mistake. But everyone dying wasn't your fault. That was the school for not putting in the safeguards. You could never have seen it coming.'

'Don't.'

'Don't what?'

'Don't make it right. We didn't have to do anything. We could have just finished school and gotten out of there. Everyone would still be alive.'

As we sat there, Melvin put his hand on George's shoulder. George wasn't expecting it and lurched backward with fright.

'How much did you hear?' George asked when he realized it was Melvin.

'Enough. The secret is out. We can stop blaming each other and accept that what happened, happened.' Melvin said. 'I'm tired of running from my past. So thank you for sharing it with Matt.'

Melvin and George stand and hug.

It was only then I realized everyone else had been watching. Listening.

'It seems like our family knows about you two and your secret. And based on the looks on everyone's faces…'I look around the room, scanning everyone's eyes. 'Your secret is safe with us.'

Everyone nods in agreement. Big smiles on their faces. They all rush in to take turns hugging both of them.

'We're back.' I say softly to myself. With a big smile on my face. 'We're a family again.'

Chapter 65

'Well everyone, let's finish...' I start to say.

ALARM!!!

'Of course there's an alarm.' I say to myself. Like it should be a big surprise.

I release a big sigh. 'Trap, how much time we got?'

'Well, I've automated the defense protocols so that we can get out while they fight to get in.' Trap paused, looked up, did some calculations in her head. 'About six hours if we don't leave.'

'And what are the chances we can actually get out of here in one ship without dying?' I ask.

'About that. I think we will likely need to use the other ships as decoys, distractions, drone defenses, and ultimately suicides.' Trap said, hoping she wouldn't get in trouble.

'Very well.' I said.

'Very well!?' Sharon shouted in surprise. 'Sir you worked your ass off to get those ships. You're just going to let them get blown up?'

'I guess now is as good a time to come clean since everyone else is.' I choke on my words. 'I don't do this job for money. I never have to worry about money. My kids will never have to worry about money. Their great-great-grand children won't have to worry about money.'

Everyone stares. Except Sharon. She knows. I think she said what she said to keep my secret. Trap also just kept a straight face. Of course she knows. She seems to know everything. Atlas probably knows just being a part of Sharon's life. I guess it was really just Melvin and George that were staring.

'I do this because I want people around me. I'm afraid of being alone. I was alone my whole life. Never really had friends because they all just used me for my money and for stuff.'

I teared up a bit but continued.

'My dad was never around because he was always busy with the business. My mom died when I was young. Too young to remember. I have been alone my whole life.'

Now they are all staring. Not just Melvin and George.

'I thought that if you knew I had money, you would become those people in my past that used me for my money. You wouldn't want to be around me for me.

Those ships don't matter. I can replace them on a whim.

This base doesn't matter. It was easy to assemble.

Building this family took work. Work! Something I've never had to actually do. And I cherish you all. I had to WORK to build this family. And I won't let us die just to keep a few ships around. I worked too hard to be with people who care about me…' And I break.

I have never cried this hard in my life. I have never cried in front of people. Tears, sure. Never crying.

I don't know how long I was crying or when it happened, but everyone was around me, hands on my shoulders, arms, legs, wherever they could make a connection. Trap in front of me, holding my hands.

I look up and at each of them in their eyes. I know without any words being spoken what each of them is thinking. I only see love in their eyes.

Except for Atlas. I still can't read the dude. Seriously. If we survive, I need to take some courses about Vantatlian facial expressions.

But here he is. With everyone else. Holding on to me.

'Thank you.' Is all I can say out loud. And in a soft voice.

I seem to be lifted in unison by everyone.

'This has been lovely. But we need to get moving.'
Sharon finally said. Everyone breaks and heads for
the Pup. Everyone except Trap.

Trap leans up and looks me in the eyes and gives me
the biggest reassuring kiss ever. 'I knew you were
rich. Remember, I know everything.' She winks,
slaps my ass, and does a little dance as she walks
away. Looking back ever so lovingly.

I love her.

Chapter 66

'Melvin. Are you good to fly?' I ask.

'Better than I have been in a long long long time sir.'

'Great. Let's go. We need to regroup and then head for the prize.'

And so we depart. Never to see Camp Adleston again.

As we get far enough away, Melvin turns the ship so we can watch.

3

That place was like the treehouse I never had growing up because we were never around trees.

2

I built a family here. It was a safe place.

1

It was my home. As much as I didn't want to admit it. It really did feel that way.

0

The brilliant glow as Camp Adleston and the Margun deleted themselves was something extraordinary. And it served two purposes. Hopefully, the HSP saw it and decided we were done for. And if not, it certainly will give them pause.

'Head for Tuck Tuck's Tomb.' I said to Melvin.

Melvin turned on the hydrox-injectors.

'Sir. Time to buckle up.' Roach said.

'Thanks for the reminder, Roach. Missed you. And hey, I brought George back to you.' I said.

'Thank you sir. I noticed.' Roach said sarcastically.

'Is anyone going to tell me what Tuck Tuck's Tomb is?' Trap asks.

'Hell no. This is a rare occasion. All of us knowing something you don't. It'll probably never happen again.' Sharon said, patting her new friend on the back.

As we approach the wormhole and the battle of HSP versus our defense system, we notice that the little exploding lights start to slow down. We must either be winning or running out of things that go boom.

'Melvin, what can you see?' I ask.

'It appears that there are only two HSP cruisers left.' Melvin said. 'The others are either rubble in space or left for repairs.'

'They left.' Roach chimed in. 'There is not enough rubble in the system for a ship to have actually been expired.'

'Thank goodness.' Trap said. 'It was never my intention to blow them up and kill people. Just send them packing.'

'Are we in the best formation for avoiding death?' I ask.

'We are.' Sharon said. 'They'll attack the first ship and second to last ship assuming that we are in one of them. The false heat signatures will throw them off as well.'

We get closer and start seeing things coming our way. Our ships break formation and two of them head towards the wormhole. The Pup, the Alpha Monkey, and the Flance head for the HSP ships.

'Are you sure this is a good idea?' George asks.

'Of course.' Sharon said. 'They'll assume the three ships heading for the HSP are a distraction, and they'll also assume the two heading for the wormhole are trying to escape. They'll break off of their current position and head for the two ships.'

'And if they don't?' Melvin asks.

'That's where Trap comes in, but that's only as a backup.' Sharon says as she winks at Trap.

And as expected. The ships break off and head for the "escaping ships."

As soon as they are clear, we head for the wormhole. It was only after they engaged the other two ships did they realize they were being played. And it is too late for them to do anything. We are out of there.

Chapter 67

We get to Tuck Tuck's Tomb a few hours later. And as you guessed it, it is another hiding place we built in another part of space that usually gets zero traffic.

A long time ago humans built a cemetery in space. At the time, they decided it was easier to leave bodies in space and "bury" them in a big spherical tomb than to ship them back to Earth. For those that didn't want to be launched into space, sent back to burn up in the atmosphere, cremated, etc.

Yeah, it existed for religious purposes.

And, as you guessed it. The project was eventually lost to time and was abandoned because of money. I had money. I bought it. Moved it here. Didn't tell anyone about it. But if anyone comes looking, they'll see what it is and bug out.

People aren't used to keeping dead bodies around. It freaks them out. Now, people shoot the bodies into a star or recycle them for plant food. Burying them is so weird to most people that they just don't even want to deal with it.

Not me. I decided to retrofit the unused parts for my personal use.

And now, here we are. Settling into a new home.

'Let's get everything unpacked, settled, retrofit the ships as needed, and go get Kip.' I said.

I get a series of acknowledgments, and everyone moves on.

I need to contact my dad and see if everything is still as it was or if the plan changed.

I walk into my room, and before I call, I remembered that this place isn't as secure as it could be. 'Trap! Can you come in here?'

I hear a bunch of Ooooo's from the crew.

'Stop being so childish. It's not like that.' I shout in return.

'Trap, I need you to make sure we are secure here. I need to contact my dad and see how things have changed before we launch. But I want to make sure we aren't tracked.'

'Give me thirty minutes and you'll be good to go.' Trap said and walked out.

'See, I told you!' I shouted as though anyone really cared.

Trap walks in, 'All good cap…' she paused…'my love.' And then walks out. Blushing.

I forgot what I was doing.

Oh yeah. Dad. Buzz kill.

I make the call. I hope all is well. I hope my dad is alive. I hope Kip is still where he is. I am questioning myself again. Dammit.

Chapter 68

'Dad. Are you there?'

He steps into the picture. His face, a bloody mess.

'I'll be speaking for your dad, you little fuck.'

'And who might you be?' I ask. Sick to my stomach and highly pissed off.

'My name is Michael Stitch. You have stolen something from me. I want it back.'

'What do you think we have? Because from what I can tell, we haven't stolen anything.' I type a quick message to Sharon to get her ass in here now.

'You fucking know what you have and what I want. You think I am playing? Here is your dad's face.' And he shoves it into view again. 'I am not playing around, and I will finish off your dad if you don't give me what I want.'

Just then, Sharon walks in.

'Ah, Sharon Marshfield. How long has it been?' Michael said as he saw her walk into view.

'Not long enough you prick.' Sharon replied.

'Should have shot you as a traitor rather than release you from service.' Michael said in return.

I thought I have seen Sharon pissed off, but her face brought fear to my grandchildren, and Trap isn't even pregnant yet.

'Before you say a fucking word, you two.' Michael interrupted. 'Give me what I want now. Or…'

'Or what!?' Sharon interrupted.

'Or this.' Michael hit my dad in the head with his fist. And pulled up another man on screen. 'Or I kill Kiping right in front of you.'

'You wouldn't.' Fuck I spoke too quickly. I didn't keep my cool.

'I would. I know you want the Pims location, and you think Kip is the answer. Well, fine. Give me what I want, and I'll give you Kip.' Michael said with conviction.

'Fuck you.' Is all that came out of my mouth.

And without a second's hesitation.

Bam!

The screen went red with Kip's head, brain, skull, and a fucking dead man standing behind what used to be Kip.

'NOOOOOOOO!!!!' I yell. I stand, grasping the screen. I shout God knows what. Sharon trying to keep me from doing something stupid.

The screen goes dark.

I drop.

'I'm going to kill him.' I said in a low hatred voice.

'No, you won't. You wouldn't be able to. But we can make him suffer.' Sharon said calmly. 'I promise.'

And I start to cry, again.

'Please tell me that my dad is going to be okay.' As I whimper into the corner holding myself together as to not fall apart.

Chapter 69

'Matt. Sweety.' Trap said as she walked in on us. 'I have something that will help.'

'What?' I ask with a sad and broken voice.

'The recording of what just transpired.'

'What good is that?'

'Michael Stitch just killed the son of the Weavel Corporation CEO. Stitch just lost all favor with the second most power corporation in the galaxy. Only he doesn't know it yet.'

'And?' Clearly I'm unable to think for myself at the moment.

'And, that means we now have an ally.'

'But what about Farenx? What about Brolian?' I ask as my mind starts working again.

'Brolian was working with Stitch to take over the Farenx Corporation. We can use that to get Walter on our side too. Then we have all three corporations against Stitch and the HSP as a whole.'

'I'm not following!' I finally shouted in frustration.

'Just trust me. I know where Trap is going with this.' Sharon said leaving the room.

'We'll make things right. I promise.' Trap said as she sits down next to me.

I sit. Tears in my eyes. But I am glad she is there.

'I'm sorry.' Trap said softly.

'For what?'

'For not letting you in sooner. I was keeping up my defenses so I wouldn't get hurt.' Trap cleared her throat. 'I also grew up with nobody. And it was easier to keep it that way than to get hurt again.'

'I…' I began to say something but decided just to listen.

'From the moment I met you, I knew there was something I liked. But I was afraid to let you know. I was afraid to let myself know. Being vulnerable isn't something I do. I almost don't know how.' Trap said. 'But I see you with your crew. I see how much they like and respect you. I see how much you all mean to each other. And I want that too. Sharon was the only thing really keeping me at bay. I thought she was in love with you too. And once we figured that out, well, I had no more excuses.'

'I'm sorry too.' I finally said. 'I screwed up a friendship by making it romantic. Lost a crew member. A family member. All because she was…'

'Married.' Trap said finishing my sentence.

'Because you know everything.' I said with a smile. And then kissed her.

Then I finished my thought, 'I didn't want to ruin another friendship. I was afraid.'

'I get it.' Trap interrupted. And kissed me again.

Chapter 70

'Okay everyone. Today we end this. Everything. The war. The corruption. The fucking Pim device debacle. Everything.' I say to the crew.

'We are going to send the device into a star. Because fuck it. At this point, nobody should have it and we can make sure of it by burning it up.'

'Not going to work. There is a flaw.' Trap said interrupting me. 'Also, I have a better plan.'

'Oh yeah? What's the flaw?'

'If we fire it at a star, the HSP has ships that can get really close to said star. And because we would have to fire off so far from the star, they would have time to get their ship in and swoop up the device.' Trap explained.

'Besides...Better plan...Did you miss that part?'

'Okay. Let's hear it.'

'I didn't want to say anything until I had it because I didn't want to get anyone's hopes up, especially mine, but Kip's death made me rethink things.'

'Go on.'

'I figured that if Kip was expendable, Stitch had to have the coordinates to the Pim home world somewhere. Not to mention that the whole trip Kip went on would have been stored somewhere.' Trap took a breath. 'I tried to find the coordinates from the trip logs, but I couldn't find them. It wasn't until Kip's death that I realized Stitch had the coordinates too. He wouldn't give up something that valuable.'

'So, you hacked the HSP and found the coordinates?' I asked

'I did indeed.'

'Then we fuck everything else that is going on and hightail it to the Pim home world. Give them the device, find our way home, and come back to a whole mess of legal and ethical issues that we won't have to solve.'

'Exactly.'

'Sounds easy enough.' I said. 'Where do we start?'

'I have broadcast signals back at my fortress. It should be uninhabited and still functional. I did make it seem like the HSP was there, but they really weren't. Again, I'm sorry about that.'

'Never mind the past. Let's get moving. I don't want to keep dancing around this shit anymore. Let's end it.' I demanded. 'And yes, we are taking the device. Either we do all of this or we don't do any of it.'

'Do or die!' Sharon shouted.

'Do or what?' Melvin shrieked.

'It's just a saying.' George said trying to reassure Melvin.

We decide it is best to return the device first since we have the coordinates. Then we can head back and fuck up everyone's reality. Safer that way.

'Here are the coordinates, Melvin.' Trap said handing them over.

'Are we really going to be meeting the Pims?' Melvin asked. 'It's always been a dream of mine to do so.'

'We'll see. I wouldn't plan on it. But that is the goal. We need to return the device.'

'Okay. I'll hold in my excitement until it happens.' Melvin said. 'Hang on tight. Here we go!'

And we enter the tunnels.

I wonder what they are like.

I wonder if they'll be happy to see the device's return.

I wonder if they'll kill us.

Fuck. Maybe I will get us all killed.

But hey, at least the rest of the galaxy won't have the device to destroy each other over.

I sit down for some coffee and a staring contest with my new love. Her eyes are like magic. I could stare at them for days.

We don't exchange words. Just looks. Giggles. Thoughts about the future. And real, honest, loving smiles.

What seemed like no time at all and I hear, 'Coming up on the exit.' Melvin said over the speakers.

'That was fast.' I mutter.

It seems like everyone is rushing into the bridge all at once. I can't blame anyone. We have never seen a Pim in our lives.

We exit. And just like every other exit, it's pretty much just space. We do a scan and see that there is a planet off in the distance. We also detect no way to get back to the wormholes. Just like Kip said.

No alarms. That's good.

'Let's head towards the planet. Keep all frequencies open.' I tell Melvin.

'Send a hello message just letting them know we are here and not trying to hide.' Sharon demanded.

'Good call.' I said.

Melvin hit the switch to send the message.

And we continue to head towards the planet.

I can see everyone is starting to be on edge. Why is nobody contacting us? Do they really think so little of us?

Just then our ship stops as we all lurch forward.

What seems like no time at all, our ship is pulled into the belly of a massive ship.

Our door opens. Nobody comes in.

'I guess that's our queue to get out of the ship.' I surmise. 'Atlas, Sharon, George, Melvin, Trap, can you grab the device and bring it with? I'll head out first and see what is happening.'

They all head for the device.

I choke down a breath.

I walk out of the ship.

Standing there is a single Pim. It is taller than Atlas by many feet. It isn't muscular though. Kind of skinny. A pale mixture of colors. Nothing I have seen that would be similar enough to capture its beauty.

The crew comes out with the device.

The Pim looks at us. Looks at the device.

I guess I go first.

'Hello. My name is Matt. My friend Kip got this device from you to get back home. It has caused a lot of problems for everyone in our system. We are here to return it.'

'Hello Matt. My name is Rebagagakah. You can call me Reb as I am sure it will be easier for you to say.'

I would ask how it knows our language, but that would be stupid. I'm sure they have their ways.

'Come on in Matt. Bring your crew. We always want our guests to feel welcome.' Reb said as he motioned towards another part of the ship.

We all walk in awe. We don't know what to say or do. This is all so surreal. The architecture is beautiful, and yet it seems to be part of the planet itself. Almost like a symbiosis of nature and its inhabitants.

I muster some focus and explain the situation to Reb.

'Matt. It pains me to hear of the pain this device has caused you. It should have deconstructed itself upon use. We will have our technicians take care of it.'

We sit and listen. We take in what is said. We marvel in this being's presence. We get a selfie. Cause nobody is going to believe this.

'Reb. We appreciate the hospitality. And I hate to be the one that pulls us away from learning about you and your people. But we have a mission. We must put an end to our wars. To our horrible lust for power. To do that, we must go back and face those who would have used this device for their own purposes.'

'If it helps persuade those in power, know this. We would rather take the tunnels away from you than see you harm one another. If you can't find a way to live in peace, we will have to take back what was given. We do know it can take time and we are patient people. We will be watching.'

'Thank you, Reb.' I say with a smile on my face before I turn to leave. 'Would it be alright if we returned some day? We have much to learn from you. I think it could help us progress as a people if we could spend more time with you.'

'Matt, you and your crew may return whenever you like.' Reb said with a smile. I think it's a smile. I'm going to say that it is. Hey, maybe I'll be the foremost expert on Pim facial expressions before I figure out if Atlas is mad, happy, or even tired.

We head back to the ship.

'Time to get back everyone.' I said to a group of people that looked like disappointed kids. 'Instead of giving us a device, Reb is going to open a temporary wormhole for us so we can return without the possibility of a defective Pim device.'

'It's for the best.' I continued.

Everyone nodded in agreement.

'Melvin, take us to Trap's place. We have a call to make.' I said with determination.

Chapter 72

'It looks intact.' Trap said. 'I'm not picking up any ships or anomalies.'

'Any stealth?' Sharon asked.

'I'm good, but not that good. If there is stealth, I don't know that I could tell.' Trap said with a bit of defeat in her voice.

'I wouldn't assume they expected us to come here, especially if they didn't know about it. Neat trick by the way. The systems all worked together to show us a ghost ship and the missiles, explosions, and the whole show.' Sharon admitted.

'Backups!' Trap said with a smile.

We land. We go inside. Trap starts working on her systems. I rehearse what I am going to say.

'We'll be connected to everyone shortly.' Trap said. 'Thirty seconds.'

'Stay calm sir. You got this. And I got your back.' Sharon said.

'I got this.' I said to myself.

'You'll do great.' George said.

'Thanks.' I said as a reaction more than actually acknowledging and understanding what was said.

'And, you're on in five seconds.'

I breath in.

I breath out.

I'm ready to change the trajectory of the galaxy.

On the various screens, I see many faces.

I see Walter, the CEO of Farenx.

I see Brolian, the VP of Farenx.

I see Darvell, the CEO of Weavel.

I see my dad.

I see Michael Stitch, hovering over my dad.

I see the Grand Irrabble of Vantatlia.

I see the head of the Morlapian people.

I even see some Splim dude. I have never seen one in the past. Not sure why I am seeing one now. Trap knows things. Must be their head guy. But I know what I need to say, and it does include the Splims.

'I come before you because the lies are too many. The corruption too great. The struggles too common.

My crew and I have been hunted for many weeks now. For what? For a single-use Pimtim device? And why?

For power. Power over the wormholes. Maybe not today, but in time. Whoever gets the device will eventually learn the secrets. And it will only be a matter of time before that power is exploited.

Many of you have been playing each other. Making deals. Stabbing each other in the back. Only to turn around and stab someone else in the back.

Holding back the truth. The truth.' I repeat for emphasis.

'We have proof that it was not the Vantatlians that destroyed the Splim homeworld. It was the Morlapians.

And it was the HSP that kept the truth from the Splims. The HSP wanted to make sure the Splims continued to attack and keep everyone's guard up. To keep up defense spending.

To stay in business.

Only this was just the beginning.

My friend Kip stumbled on the Pimtim's home world. He found a wormhole that entered their system but didn't leave. Kip received the return device, which everyone is vying for, from the Pimtims in order to get back home. The Pimtims knew it was single use, and it was supposed to deconstruct itself after use.

You might be wondering how we know. How a small crew knows this information. We returned the device to its rightful owners. We met the Pimtims. We learned the truth from these fantastic beings. Beings with compassion and understanding.

They wanted to open our eyes to the universe. They did not want us to hurt each other. And if we don't figure out how to get along, they will take from us that which we have grown to take advantage of. Proof of our meeting with the Pimtims is being transmitted.

But I am only getting started.

You see, Kip knew what he had and told his father. The Weavel Corporation took the device to hopefully use the power for themselves. Only Brolian knew something was up as Kip worked for the Farenx Corporation charting the wormhole system. Since there are more corporate spies than military spies, it didn't take long before Brolian figured out where the device was and how to get it to Farenx instead.

Brolian got the transfer order in through his spy network. They used my crew and me to move it from one location to another. They did this so that if anything went wrong, everyone could blame my father and take him for his entire net worth and take his company as their own. Of course, Walter didn't know anything about this as Brolian kept the information to himself so he could take over Farenx with the help of Michael Stitch.

Only Stitch had his own plans for galactic domination. He would use whoever he could to get the device, learn its secrets, and then take out whoever he saw to be an obstacle. He was tired of taking orders from the top and wanted to start being at the top.

We got deeply involved when we took a wrong turn and saw the Canvern talking with the Morlapians and Splims. We didn't understand why at the time, but Stitch had convinced the two to stand down just long enough to promise them everything they ever wanted.

He promised that the Morlapians would get Vantatlian worlds in exchange for their support.

He promised the Splims that they would get revenge on the Vantatlians for destroying their home world. Extending the lie. Keeping the Splims from ever learning the truth that it was the Morlapians who destroyed their home world.

The Morlapians have always wanted to take over planets for resources. But after the battle over their home world. It will take years for them to rebuild.

Wouldn't it just be easier to accept a peace treaty?'

I see everyone trying to get a word in. I see everyone angry. Confused. Talking to their aids over their shoulders. Shouting orders to whoever is in earshot. We are only receiving their pictures, not their words. They can't argue with me or each other.

They can only listen. I love it.

'The sad conclusion to this mess is that my friend Kip was murdered in front of my eyes by Michael Stitch. We recorded the whole event. We will transmit now.'

Darvell's eyes went wide. He couldn't believe what he had just heard. He couldn't believe what he was seeing. He averted his eyes. And then said something over his shoulder. I'm assuming to some confidant. He looks pissed. I'm sure Stitch won't survive much longer after this transmission.

'You are definitely asking yourself how we know these things? How a small crew could come by all of these facts? A man named Peter from Designation 13 had most of the information but couldn't put all of the pieces of the puzzle together. And he gave us the information he had. We are transmitting his report now.

To fill in the blanks and put the puzzle together, we have Becky to thank for that.'

I look over my shoulder. She doesn't give me the evil eye. Just a big smile. Like hearing her name actually meant something significant.

'She is the most brilliant and most talented person I know. She has information the rest of us only wish we had. I know the heads of every government, every corporation, every species would love to have her reporting to them. But that wouldn't make her the person she is today. We are transmitting her findings to you as well.

You will be able to confirm our findings. Confirm who needs to go to jail. And who should be tried for treason.'

I take a deep breath.

'To the Splims. To the Vants. To the honest leftovers of the HSP. To the corporation heads. And, yes, even the Morlapians. I ask, and the Pimtims ask, that you find peace. That you find a way to work together. There is much rebuilding to be done. There is so much we can learn from each other. There is no more need for fighting because fighting will cause us to lose everything.

We can help the Morlapians and Splims find new worlds. The galaxy is vast. We have the resources. We can even ask the Pimtims for help.'

I pause. I look around the room at my crew.

'I nearly lost my family. My crew. The people that matter most to me.

I can't imagine losing access to the entire galaxy. And I don't want to see that become a reality.

Let's not give the Pimtims a reason to take away that which keeps us from being alone in this galaxy.

We all, together, are too important to be apart.'

And with that. We end the transmission.

Epilogue

'Melvin. Here is the raise you were bitching about. As well as a bonus.' I said as I handed him a payment chip.

'Holy shit dude! Seriously!?' Melvin shouted. 'Woohoo!!!'

I walk over the George. 'You too. You deserve it.'

'Fuck me. Are you serious!?' George said and left his mouth open in disbelief.

'Sharon, this is for you.'

'Now I know what all of the cussing and excitement is about sir. I concur with Melvin and George.' Sharon said. 'And thank you. I appreciate it.'

'Atlas. I know you don't need it. But it couldn't hurt to have it. Here you go.'

'Thank you, sir.' Atlas said without even looking at it. 'I appreciate you and will always be a part of this crew.' And yeah. That's a smile. I think. Fuck he is hard to read.

'Trap.'

'Call me Becky.'

'Are you sure?'

'You're the only one that gets to call me that. Just so you know.'

'Becky it is.' I said with a smile. I guess I AM the lucky one who gets to call her Becky. 'I don't know if you need it or want it, but here you go. You deserve it.'

'I don't need it or want it. I actually have more money than you do.'

'I'm not even going to ask.'

'Nor should you.' Trap said with a grin as she turned, raised one leg behind her, grabbed my face, and gave me a kiss while I held her hips.

'Drink up everyone! It's not every person in the galaxy that gets to visit the beaches of the Pim home world.' I raise my glass.

'Maybe we can teach them how to drink.' Melvin added.

We all laugh.

'To Matt.' Melvin said curtly.

'To Matt. A great guy.' George added.

'To Matt. A great leader.' Sharon included.

'To Matt. A man I will follow.' Atlas said.

'To family!' I say, trying to get a word in.

'To Matt. A great lover.' Trap said as everyone else blushed, turned their heads, and took their drinks. I decided to kiss Trap instead of drinking to the toast.

The Wrong Turn

By Ben Winter

ISBN: 978-0-9992944-8-2